Shamayel Roidel embodies a remarkable blend of intellect and creativity, both in her literary pursuits and across every facet of her life. With an unwavering commitment to excellence, she navigates the complexities of academia, society, and personal growth with grace and determination.

Her debut work, born from a serendipitous moment of inspiration, stands as a testament to her profound dedication and clear-sighted ambition. Through its pages, Shamayel deftly weaves together insight and narrative, offering readers a glimpse into her vibrant intellect and the values that guide her journey.

Beyond her literary accomplishments, Shamayel is recognized for her forward-thinking perspective and powerful presence, qualities that have undoubtedly shaped her path to success. With each word penned and every idea realized, she continues to inspire and captivate audiences, leaving an indelible mark on the literary landscape.

I dedicate this book to those who believe in themselves in any situation and strive for success and a better life.

I dedicate it to those who sincerely loved me and supported me.

Shamayel Roidel

NEW BEGINNING

AUSTIN MACAULEY PUBLISHERS
LONDON · CAMBRIDGE · NEW YORK · SHARJAH

Copyright © Shamayel Roidel 2024

The right of Shamayel Roidel to be identified as author of this work has been asserted by author in accordance with Federal Law No. (7) of UAE, year 2002, concerning Copyrights and Neighboring Rights.

All rights reserved. No part of this publication may be reproduced, stored in a retrieval system, or transmitted in any form or by any means, electronic, mechanical, photocopying, recording, or otherwise, without the prior permission of the publishers.

Any person who commits any unauthorized act in relation to this publication may be liable to legal prosecution and civil claims for damages.

ISBN 9789948746232 (Paperback)
ISBN 9789948746225 (E-Book)

Application Number: MC-10-01-5160562
Age Classification: E

The age group that matches the content of the books has been classified according to the age classification system issued by the UAE Media Council.

Printer Name: iPrint Global Ltd
Printer Address: Witchford, England

First Published 2024
AUSTIN MACAULEY PUBLISHERS FZE
Sharjah Publishing City
P.O Box [519201]
Sharjah, UAE
www.austinmacauley.ae
+971 655 95 202

I want to talk about someone who never lost her faith and realized that to be successful, you have to try and start trying.

From the one who, in the most difficult crisis, even though she felt broken, decided to continue her way because she believed in success. Yes, I thank myself first of all for fighting.

I am grateful to my parents for supporting me and believing in me, and to my friends who accompanied me on this path and always made me feel good and told me that I can do it.

CHAPTER ONE

Moon: Beginning of new days? I don't know.
But I am trying to hope because it's the only thing can I do…
In this situation again, I tried to get out from these repetitive and tormenting thoughts because tomorrow is my birthday and I know is not a good time to be sad.
But what should I do?
Are our problems only one or two?
Definitely not…
With all of these problems and troubles, birthday doesn't have any meaning in my opinion.
My mother, my father? About my birthday?
I don't know but I feel their opinion is differently from me
OMG, look at the clock.
Yes, it's late and as usual like always, hours passed and I had strange feelings.
Oh, what is this?
Gold human? It's unbelievable.
But is not the first time.
Dream or real?

Oh, I have bad headaches. What? I think I heard my mother's voice. I'm coming.

Mother: Good morning. Oh, what a delicious breakfast! Everything is okay, my lovely daughter?

Moon: I don't know.

Mother: Why?

Moon: Because I have some strange feeling.

Mother: About?

Moon; I see some humans but they are golden. And I heard some voices from stranger people.

Mother: Oh, it's is unbelievable.

Moon: Yes, I know… I don't know. Wait, I will bring for you some medicine.

Moon: Thanks, Mom.

Mother: Here you are.

Moon: Mom?

Mother: Yes?

Moon: Where's Dad?

Mother: Work, work, and work… like always.

Moon: Yes. But I'm tired.

Mother: I know.

Moon: I have many dreams for my future, but we are in a bad situation.

Mother: It's gonna be okay.

Moon: I hope.

Mother: Okay, now go and sleep, because we have so many work to do.

Moon: Works?

Mother: I said go and sleep.

Moon: Okay, Mom. I went to my room and rested and then I heard voices.

Mother: Happy birthday, happy birthday.

Moon: Oh, Mom, dad.

Mother: Happy birthday. We wish you all the best, my girl.

Moon: Thanks, dad. I love you. Mom, I really needed this happiness.

Dad: Yes, we know.

Moon: Again, thanks for everything.
I can't lie. I expected it and now I'm happy but again me and overthinking.
I dislike this feeling, and I'm unsure how to shake it off. Perhaps I should learn to adapt. Anyway, now I need a positive vibe. Maybe I'll make a coffee while listening to music. Or better yet, both—yes, this is the right idea.
Mom?

Mother: Yes. What happened again?

Moon: Nothing. I what ice.

Mother: Check in the refrigerator.

Moon: Yes, I found it.

Julie: Hello.

Moon: Oh my god! How are you? Please leave me. Please, I was saying this with a screaming voice.

Mother: Everything is okay?

Moon: No, Mom, no. I'm seeing strange things.

Mother: What? But I don't see; maybe you need to sleep or you are tired.

Moon: You think I'm lying.

Mother: No.

Moon: It was at this moment that my mother left.

Julie: Why are you afraid?

Moon: Fear and horror.

Julie: I also said why? Because this is not correct answer.

Moon: Because it's scary.

Julie: Okay, I accepted we are Abraham.

Moon: Abraham? Before I heard it, but I don't know what it is.

Julie: We are from unseen beings.

Moon: Really??

Julie: Yes, I'm Julie with my sisters, Kathy, and Mel.

Moon: Extremely strange and incredible.

Mel: We are here to help you.

Moon: To help me?

Julie: Yes.

Moon: But about what?

Mel: Your dreams and goals. We know you were surprised and shocked.

Moon: Yes, yes, but I have one question. Where do you live?

Kathy: Above the sky and on the clouds.

Moon: Oh God! Are you serious with me?

Mel: Yes, we have land.

Moon: Can you explain more because I'm confused?

Julie: Yes, of course. You know, we have two lands, one for good, one for bad Abrahams.

Moon: We have bad Abrahams?

Julie: Yes, everywhere we see good and bad.

Moon: Yes, you are right.

•*Transition: After two hours*•

Julie: I think now you are convinced and tomorrow we can talk again. So good night, Moon.

Moon: It was an interesting conversation. And then, I went to my bedroom. I was still shocked. Is it really possible? I kept asking myself questions. Oh, I have a terrible headache again. I think I should have a coffee and after that sleep. That's how the days passed and I was still shocked.

Oh, I haven't told my mother yet. Should I tell her? I don't know. Oh, I am confused again. But I have to try. Yes.

Mother: Hi, my girl.

Moon: Hello, Mom. I wanted to say something.

Mother: Okay, tell me.

Moon: Someone spoke to me.

Mother: But who?

Moon: They are from the unseen world.

Mother: Unseen world? I don't understand what you are saying.

Moon: Wait until I explain properly.

Mother: Okay, my dear.

Moon: And I explained something about them to my mother.

Mother: It is interesting and strange.

Moon: Yes, I know and I'm still in shock.

Mother: Don't tell anyone about this.

Moon: It's a good point.

Mother: Now I have some works another time we talk about it, okay?

Moon: Okay, Mom, no problem.

Mother: But as I said, don't tell this story to anyone.

Moon: Now five months have passed since that day and I have three lovely friends. They give me different advice in various fields like studying, exercising, entertainment, and I love them.

Julie? Kathy? Mel?

Madusi: Hello moon

Moon: What? Who are you?

Madusi: I'm Abraham

Moon: I can't trust you, because I don't know anything about you.

Madusi: Because we also have good and bad sides?

Moon: Yes, but oh, I feel confused again and I don't know what's going on.

Madusi: I explain for you, I will prove to you that I am on the positive and good side and my name is Madusi. But I am here to tell you something else.

Moon: About what?

Madusi: Your real family.

Moon: What? My real family? It's impossible.

Madusi: I know you are confused but this is the truth, and this is also about your parents and this is your life but also is not your life.

Moon: The words you say are very interesting and confusing at the same time.

Madusi: Yes, I know, but you will understand better incomplete.

Moon: You know, I always knew that I was in the wrong place and time, and one day everything becomes easy.

Madusi: I want to disagree with you. You know that the difficulties and problems with this story and the things I am telling you are not going to end because this is part of our life.

Moon: And I was listening carefully to what he was saying and thinking about how accurate and accurate he was.

Madusi: Everything is okay?

Moon: between yes and not, but I am eager to know more But also I have a strange feeling. Is it normal?

Madusi: Yes and I have some works with you.

Moon: Work? With me?

Madusi: Yes, about your family because you can see them.

Moon: Are you kidding?

Madusi: No.

Moon: Oh, I want to communicate with them, please tell me how.

Madusi: Be patient; you will understand. But there is one important thing; don't talk to anyone about what I told you, even your mother.

Moon: But why?? She's my mother.

Madusi: Your question… answer is patience.

Moon: Okay, I'll try to be patient. We had interesting conversations and talked about many topics in this one week.

Madusi: Hi, Moon, I hope you have a good day.

Moon: Hi, my dear Madusi.

Madusi: So everything is good?

Moon: Between yes and no. But you said I will meet them. I talk about my family.

Madusi: Yes, I said, and you met them in a dream when you were sleeping and this is a reason for your headache. And now is the time to tell your mother about them.

Moon: Does she have the necessary capacity?

Madusi: It depends on you.

Moon: But I'm ready. Now go down and tell her and be ready for any reaction.

Moon: Madusi was right, under any circumstances I should have talked to my mother so I went to the kitchen and called my mother.

Mommy: Mom?

Mother: Yes sweetheart. Be calm please. Breakfast is ready.

Moon: Yummy, but breakfast is not important now because I want talk to you about something important.

Mother: Say it.

Moon: Mom, we have another family. Or maybe I should say real family. Are you kidding me? It's impossible.

Moon: Mommy, let me explain it for you. I spent half an hour talking and explaining to my mother, but I don't know.

Mother: I do not know what to say.

Moon: I know it's hard. I was also shocked at first, but it's true.

Mother: I need time to understand it well. No problem.

Moon: Oh, tomorrow is your day off, yes?

Mother: Yes, but I want to rest because I'm so tired.

Moon: But you promised me.

Mother: I know, but I want you to understand the situation we are in, I promise to compensate you.

Moon: Everyone wants me to understand them, but no one understands me

Mother: Sometimes you are really thoughtless and rude.

Moon: Nothing happens with a little happiness. You don't understand what I'm saying, so go to your room and think about your mistakes. Of course, I can't promise you, but maybe we will go out for the New Year celebration

Moon: I went back to my room and I constantly blamed myself for bringing it up with my mom.

Madusi: Hi, did you tell her? Wait, why are you crying?

Moon: Because she was shocked and she couldn't believe it, And we discussed.

Madusi: You had a similar behavior when you understood the story and I told you that understanding requires patience.

Moon: I don't know anything.

Madusi: And this is your biggest mistake.

CHAPTER TWO

Moon: Yes, everyone believes that I am always wrong.

Madusi: What are you saying? Let me explain to you what your mistake is.

Moon: Sorry, I'm just a little upset.

Madusi: No problem, now listen to me. Your mistake is that you think everyone understands this matter in a short time. I think you forgot, but exactly when Julie spoke to you, you were so shocked and it took time to understand.

Moon: Yes, I know it takes time, but I still feel bad.

Madusi: I have a suggestion to make you feel better.

Moon: I have no idea about it.

Madusi: Trust me. My idea is let's decorate your room in Christmas style together.

Moon: But we need Christmas things to do this.

Madusi: I know what we have to do because I have a magic wand.

Moon: Magic wand? It's unbelievable!

Madusi: Close your eyes and open them when I say.

Moon: Okay.

Madusi: I start counting one, two, three, four… And now you can open your eyes.

Moon: Oh my God! What a beautiful room! What a beautiful décor! I love you, Madusi.

Madusi: I hope you like it.

Moon: I don't like it; I love it.

Madusi: Your happiness is my happiness, my friend.

Moon: Maybe I didn't treat you well at first, but now I'm happy that you're here.

Madusi: Look at the clock.

Moon: How quickly time passes and this is strange to me. Anyway, thank you again and good night.

Madusi: Good night, see you tomorrow.

Moon: I woke up and I looked at the clock. It was almost 12 and I saw that my phone's alarm rang several times. I thought to myself, *If my mother sees me, we might argue.* That's why I decided to turn on my laptop and watch videos.

Madusi: Do you think this is the right thing to do?

Moon: Good morning, Madusi. Honestly, I don't know. Maybe I am convincing myself that I am not that kind of person.

Madusi: What kind of person do you think you are?

Moon: Sometimes I feel careless, lazy and do not understand my surroundings.

Madusi: The important thing is whether you have such thoughts or is it the behavior of the people around you that caused it.

Moon: Both.

Madusi: But most of you are the cause of these thoughts.

Moon: I want to become a better person and learn many things, but I don't know how.

Madusi: I am here to help you. You are not alone in your way

Mother: My daughter? Moon?

Moon: Mom, come in.

Mother: Hi sweetie. Wow, it's unbelievable. I love your room décor.

Moon: Madusi helped me.

Mother: Interesting and cool! I wanted to apologize to you, and also to say that we are going out next week for the New Year celebration.

Moon: Really? I wanna hug you. You are the best mother. I was very happy and we sat with my mother and talked about Madusi. It was at that moment that her phone rang and she went downstairs.

Madusi: Everything is fine?

Moon: I want to scream with joy. Because my Mom said she planned for the New Year celebration.

Madusi: I became happy.

Moon: I counted the days and nights until New Year's night And I promised myself to be happy tonight.

Julie: Madusi, shut up?

Madusi: No.

Mel: Rude boy.

Madusi: Me? Rude? No.

Julie: Yes.

Moon: What's going on here? Oh, my lovely girls.

Julie: We hate Madusi.

Moon: Sorry, I can't control my laughing.

Madusi: They are clowns.

Moon: I said that I have a phobia.

Julie: Careless.

Madusi: I have nothing to say.

Moon: Tonight is New Year, so enough. Look at Kathy. She's a good girl.

Julie: Thank you.

Moon: Oh God! I said enough, okay?

Madusi: Okay.

Moon: I feel calm now. Every day that passes I think about how they are interesting and funny creatures and they have a sweet character.

Mother: Moon, are you ready?

Moon: Yes Mommy.

Mother: Let's go together.

Moon: I feel happy.

Mother: The New Year celebration always conveys a good feeling.

Moon: Yes, I agree with you. Finally, after a busy road and traffic, we reached the place of celebration.

Mother: Wow, look at that big countdown.

Moon: Big and Beautiful.

Mother: I think it's new because I have never seen it before.

Moon: Yes, I agree with you.

Madusi: Hello Moon.

Moon: You are talking in my brain?

Madusi: Before yes, now no.

Moon: So that's why I had a headache.

Madusi: Sorry.

Moon: No problem.
Now enjoy it.

Madusi: I love this beautiful city.

Moon: City of dreams but without money. I don't know how we live here.

Mother: Now is not the time, but here is not only rich people's city and who says we don't have anything?

Moon: Sorry Mom.

Mother: Try to be worthy.

Moon: Yes, you are right.

Madusi: My friend, don't be sad. Let's enjoy together.

Moon: I agree with you. I will try to be happy tonight.

Mother: My daughter, the main ceremony of the New Year has begun.

Moon: I am watching how beautiful it is.

Madusi: Everyone counting the last ten seconds together.

Moon: One of my favorite things about New Year.

Madusi: I love all celebrations.

Moon: Me too, and happy new year, Madusi.

Mother: Happy new year, my girl.

Moon: I love you, my lovely mom.

Madusi: I hope you have a good and successful year.

Moon: You too and thank you for being my best friend.

Madusi: I think in New Year, we have a lot of adventures.

Moon: Good or bad? Or maybe both.

Madusi: Both.

Moon: Am I ready?

Madusi: I think yes and I explain it for you.

Moon: Mom, can you hear his voice?

Mother: No.

Moon: How? I thought you could hear her voice.

Madusi: We talk about it.

Moon: It was interesting and I was confused again. I was thinking about it on the way, and when I went to my room and wanted to sleep, I heard Madusi's voice: 'What are you talking about? Are you crazy?'

Madusi: My curious friend.

Moon: You know me well.

Madusi: Yes. Okay. What is your question?

Moon: I have two questions. But first second one.

Madusi: Let's talk about it.

Moon: I like to communicate and talk with my family and I wanna go to see them.

CHAPTER THREE

Madusi: But they are not here.

Moon: I don't understand, but you said to help me to know them

Madusi: I said, yes, but if they were here, so what is the cause of your dreams? This is a sign that they are not present where we are.

Moon: Another city or country?

Madusi: No, they are living on second Earth.

Moon: What? Enough. I can't believe. What is the second Earth?

Madusi: But I'm not lying because we really have a parallel Earth.

Moon: How strange and complicated!

Madusi: I know, people think it doesn't exist, but, who go there all the time, knows that there is second Earth. Maybe it's hard. And some people think that we are lying.

Moon: I didn't say you are lying, but I find it hard to believe Because I didn't think about these things until now and I didn't know that such a thing could exist. And you must understand me.

Madusi: You're right. I was nervous because I thought you wouldn't believe me, but now you've proven to me with your words that you're looking for the truth and you want to know, so I'll tell you everything you need to know, but it might take years.

Moon: You know, I don't want to say anything that you might misunderstand, but everything is strange and somehow incomprehensible to me.

Madusi: Understand what you're saying. That's why I said it takes years because you have to grow, evolve, and come to real understanding.

Moon: Yes, you are right. This process takes time, and I…

Madusi: Now I wanna say something.

Moon: About what?

Madusi: I am going to stay here.

Moon: Stay with me? First good news of the year?

Madusi: You don't have any problems?

Moon: Of course, no, I'm happy to have a knowledgeable and funny friend like you. Well, enough talking, I'll go get the vacuum cleaner. I was supposed to put the laziness aside and tidy up my room.

Madusi: But this thing you have is not a room, more like an Amazon Forest.

Moon: Very ridiculous, at least come and help me instead of these words.

Madusi: I can't do anything. Just eat.

Moon: Oh God! You are so funny.

Madusi: Thank you.

Moon: I'm going to start tidying up here, so I hope the noise doesn't bother you.

Madusi: Don't worry. I'm not bothered and I feel comfortable.

Moon: Good.

And two and a half hours passed.

Madusi: No, I really have to plan for you.

Moon: Plan? For me?

Madusi: Yes, In order to make you, who care so much about cleaning your surroundings, out of laziness and turn into someone who is very interested in these things and tidying up.

Moon: No, look, it's not like you say that I don't do much, but if I start, I won't stop until it's neat, and now I feel that I've reached this stage.

Madusi: Can't you hear the sound of the room door?

Moon: Oh, I think my mom said that she will make juice and bring it.

Mother: Hi, my daughter. Hello, Mom, what do you think about my room Now?

Mother: It's great, you can be so orderly. Why don't you do it?

Moon: This is a big question even for me, but I will try to pay more attention from now on.

Mother: Well done, that's exactly what I wanted to hear. After you've had your juice, get ready. We're going out.

Moon: Are you kidding?

Mother: I'm not kidding you. The best time to go out together and have fun is after the new year ceremony and fireworks.

Moon: Oh, thanks, Mom. That was the best thing I could hear.

Mother: I knew you would be happy, so I will go down.

Moon: Okay, I'm going to change my clothes. Wow, Madusi, Madusi, wow, wow!

Madusi: What happened? I left the room for some minutes.

Moon: My mom said that we are going out to see the ceremony for the new year. I am very happy.

Madusi: I was waiting for her to say, so she finally said.

Moon: Well, let me see, did you know that she was going to say this?

Madusi: Yes, because I have the power of mind reading and I can do it.

Moon: How interesting! You are beyond a being with extraordinary powers and every day you tell me something new about yourself that makes me wonder.

Madusi: I did not know that you would be so surprised, of course there are more things that you will understand in the future.

Moon: Let me tell you; I'm excited to find out.

Madusi: So keep that excitement because you are not going to understand right now.

Moon: But since I am ready, why not now?

Madusi: I think you forgot, but I said that this understanding and growth takes time and you will realize many things over the years. Now go, get ready, we're going to go out and have some much needed fun.

Moon: You're right, you told me all this before, so I'll go get ready

•Transition: *Half an hour passed*•

Mother: My daughter, where are you?

Moon: I'm ready, Mom. Shall we go?

Mother: Let's go, but we have to see if we will arrive on time with this delay.

Moon: Please don't complain now. Let one night pass peacefully and jokingly. For example, it's almost New Year, so we should be happy.

Mother: You always know what to say to calm my anger.

Moon: Well, this is one of my secret techniques that I don't tell anyone.

Mother: So you also know such things.

Moon: Of course, I know because I have a good guide.

Mother: Remember to tell me more about your guides. I'm curious to know a lot about it.

Moon: We will definitely talk to each other when we have the opportunity, because there are many things that will definitely shock you at first, but gradually it becomes believable.

Mother: So I was more eager to hear and know.

Moon: How interesting! Oh, Mom, we arrived, it's so crowded. I wish we had left earlier.

Mother: Then you say don't grumble and don't complain. It's worth a quarter of an hour. The earlier we came, it would definitely be better, but as you say, let's not spoil the night and enjoy.

Moon: Thank God that you liked my techniques and I was able to help. Oh Mom, how many minutes are left?

Mother: Just 10 Minutes.

Moon: Mom Look there, we can go. Let me see, yes, it's a good place. Let's go soon. Take objection from me but you can and see what pure ideas I have.

Mother: Hey, what's wrong with you? I'm telling you, in addition to being so good, pay more attention, be careful, and don't forget order.

Moon: Sorry Mom, as I said, I promise, but now let's enjoy the ceremonies that are about to start.

Madusi: Hello, I'm here too.

Moon: Where have you been? Do you know how worried I was about you?

Madusi: Oh, it means I became an important person.

Moon: How many minutes are left? Don't bother me. Tell me where you were.

Madusi: I decided to come by myself, but I had a problem. I'm late. I'm sorry. But now I feel like I became an important person.

Moon: It's obvious that it's important. Well, you're my friend and you mean a lot to me. So, are you going somewhere or do you want to come later? Tell me not to worry.

Mother: Sweetie, be calm and don't talk to yourself so much in public.

Moon: Mom no.

Mother: I know, I know, but speak calmly. Others will be surprised and think you are crazy.

Moon: Okay, Mom, I'm sorry, I'm trying to speak calmly.

Madusi: Oh, how I hate it! People are so crazy.

Moon: My friend, calm down. You told me yourself that most people still don't understand such creatures like you.

Madusi: Yes, I said it and it's true, but I got nervous and felt that I was hit.

Moon: Well, don't worry, we will go eat after the ceremony.

Madusi: You know how to make me happy. I am happy now.

Mother: Moon?

Moon: Yes, Mom.

Mother: Look there, it's starting. If you didn't want us to come out, then let's go home.

Moon: Sorry, I got distracted.

Mother: Later I talk to you about it. Now enjoy it.

Moon: Okay Mom. Oh my God! The countdown.

Mother: Let's repeat with it.

Moon: And Happy New Year.

Mother: Happy New Year, my daughter. May the best things happen to us!

Moon: I hope it will be like this.

Madusi: I wish you the best and I hope you will be one step closer to your dreams in New Year.

Moon: Thank you, my friend. Mom, did you hear what Madusi said?

Mother: No, honestly, I don't hear his voice and I don't notice his presence.

Moon: But I thought you would understand and see it.

Moon: Oh, this is another strange thing that happened.

Mother: But it doesn't matter so much, as long as you talk to him and he is present, we should be thankful.

Moon: It is definitely so and this is a very important point that was mentioned.

Mother: Yes, my dear.

Moon: Just as I was thinking, I asked what time it was.

Madusi: Almost two in the morning.

Moon: You must be joking, Madusi.

Madusi: No, by the way, I was quite serious.

Moon: How quickly time passes and it's strange.

Mother: But, my daughter, the important thing is that we had so much fun that we didn't realize it. If you look at it from this angle, you will see that it happened for a good reason, and what do you think?

Moon: Yes, you are exactly right and we should look at the story in this way so that we can enjoy life.

Madusi: Your mother is right. Don't get too carried away. Why did it happen like this? Live in the present, even if sometimes it's hard, so when you feel good, be thankful and enjoy it so you can see and feel more moments like this.

Moon: And it was after hearing those words that I came to my senses again and felt that yes, I really should be able to enjoy life. Last night was the best opportunity to understand many things again, but there is still one question that is occupying my mind. Surely, why doesn't your mother hear my voice or notice my presence?

Moon: Yes, that's exactly my question, and you read my mind again, what I want to say.

Madusi: Well, look, as I said before, many things take time. Even this story could be the other way around, so look. There is every possibility.

Moon: Yes, I know these things, but I want to get the answer to my question, why can't he hear your voice?

Madusi: You will understand, but not now, but in the very near future.

Moon: So there are a lot of things I'm going to figure out.

Madusi: True, but that day will come and you will realize everything in the most real way. And many days passed like this until the New Year holidays ended and now it was time for schools to reopen and people to go back to work. And I was drowning in these thoughts when I noticed his presence by my mother's voice.

Mother: Moon, starting tonight, you should sleep early and pay more attention to your studies.

Moon: Yes, I know, but Mom, can I have my phone?

Mother: Yes, but there are conditions put the phone away at a certain time, it will also focus on useful things.

Moon: Okay, I know, you don't need to tell me so much, I'm going to study for tomorrow's exam.

Mother: Proud of you. Sweetheart, be careful not to break that glass. Oh my God, I told you to be careful, but it's not clear what you were thinking that made you so distracted.

Moon: Mom, you shouldn't have left the glass like that, it wasn't my fault.

Mother: No, it's not like you don't understand. In addition to what I said, I'll also add that you don't accept your mistake. I don't know when you're going to learn these things. Maybe you never want to understand, and this is always the way to escape from the truth.

Moon: I'm sorry, I made a mistake, but I shouldn't be treated like this. It makes me feel like a fool I want to be alone.

Madusi: Are you okay?

Moon: Do you think this is the right question you are asking?

Madusi: No, I understand, I made a mistake, sorry.

Moon: Do not pay attention to such words.

CHAPTER FOUR

Moon: How can I not pay attention; I really do not understand why I am being treated like this.

Madusi: If you want, you can talk to me.

Moon: We'll talk later. Now I have to go to sleep. Tomorrow, we have school.

Madusi: Good night.

Moon: Oh God! I still feel like I need to sleep.

Madusi: I know how you feel but you have to get over it. So don't delay and get ready for school.

Moon: The second version of my mother.

Madusi: What? She can't talk to me.

Moon: Yes, you are right and now is not the time to argue and fight. I have to go and do my work. At the same time, I heard my mother's voice and went towards her.

Mother: Moon, where are you moon?

Moon: Yes Mom.

Mother: I thought you didn't wake up. Let's go now, my dear.

Moon: Madusi, let's go to school together.

Madusi: You made me happy.

Moon: Oh, my lovely little friend.

Madusi: Well, don't talk too much here, otherwise they will think I'm crazy.

Moon: Thank you for reminding me, but I am careful. But I missed the school atmosphere and my friends and now I am happy.

Sanaz: Moon moon, heyyy!

Moon: My dear Sanaz, I missed you so much.

Sanaz: Me too, did you have a good vacation?

Moon: It wasn't bad, I was mostly at home, but I'm used to it.

Sanaz: I also didn't go anywhere as much and I was mostly at home.

Moon: Markar talking to whom?

Sanaz: She is telling the memories of her vacations.

Moon: Sometimes I doubt justice. Even in this city, there are places that I haven't been to, then she went on European trips.

Sanaz: Don't be sad. Don't look at your position. One day, you will get what you want.

Moon: Yes, you are right and thank you for supporting me so much.

Sanaz: You are my best friend. Let's go and talk in the yard until the class starts.

Moon: I love your ideas.

Sanaz: Oh, look there. Marmar is coming towards us. Look, relax and act normal because you know that she wants to disturb your peace.

Marmar: Hello girls, I missed you two. What did you do on vacation?

Moon: Thank you, I'm fine. If I want to be honest with you, I have to tell you that I was busy.

Marmar: Oh, so you didn't go anywhere? Of course, this is not a good question because I know the answer.

Sanaz: Our family decided to go to the forest and camp.

Marmar: Going to the forest and camping is very good, but for you, it is not attractive for me. Oh, that class is about to start. Let's go before it's too late see you.

Sanaz: Oh God, I can't.

Moon: You told me to be calm, so do it yourself.

Sanaz: Yes, I said it, but she is very selfish and rude.

Moon: Leave it and let's go. We have an exam today, right?

Sanaz: Yes, literature exam.

Moon: Severe stress.

Sanaz: Don't worry, we have two classes with Mrs. Smith today. Maybe she will let us review and then she will take the test.

Mrs. Smith: Hello my girls, I'm glad to see you again.

Moon: We are also happy, teacher.

Mrs. Smith: Hi, I hope your mind's is ready.

Moon: Are we going to write an essay?

Mrs. Smith: Oh, Moon, you are very smart and this is exactly what I want. Yes, this is your first exam after vacation. I will give you a bunch of topics and you can choose any one you want. Of course, I don't want a very long essay either. I am looking for the concept and this is important to me.

Moon: And Mrs. Smith wrote the topics one after another on the board and dedicated the class that day to this topic.

Sanaz: Everything is okay, Moon?

Moon: Yes, don't worry, I was thinking about what to write about. You know I have doubts between three topics. New Year and holiday, science is better or wealth, maybe dreams.

Sanaz: I think it's very good that you write about dreams, of course you know that I like your writings.

Moon: I liked your advice.

Sanaz: Well, you are my friend, I should be able to help you.

Moon: What's your subject?

Sanaz: Family camping in forest.

Moon: Wow, I am waiting to hear your essay.

Sanaz: Thanks, but you know Mrs. Smith is right, you are very smart, but one thing is strange to me.

Moon: Come to our house in the evening after school and I will tell you.

Sanaz: Okay, I will definitely tell my mother and I will come.

Moon: I started writing and tried to observe the details in my writing.

Mrs. Smith: Well, my girls, have you finished writing?

Marmar: Can I come and read?

Mrs. Smith: My dear Marmar, I am eager to hear what you wrote and let's talk about your topic.

Marmar: Wealth or science? Which one is better?

Sanaz: But what do you think she wrote?

Moon: You don't have to ask me, I think you should better understand what he wrote about her wealth and definitely her family.

Sanaz: Yes, I know, but Mrs. Smith also has his own policies.

Moon: After a few minutes, Mrs. Smith spoke about the Marmar essay and she was so precise that I was thinking that she is one of our best teachers.

Mrs. Smith: Exceptionally, only two essays can be read in this session. Who is next?

Moon: Shall I come and read? Of course, my dear, I am eager to hear and tell about the topic you wrote about.

Moon: My topic is about dreams.

Mrs. Smith: We hear very well.

Moon: We have many dreams and we usually talk about them, but we rarely look for the right way to achieve them, and we just talk about it, but I don't think so. And in my opinion, we should try to achieve our desires and even if we fail, we should continue again and not leave the path because many things may happen along the way, but it is very important to try and resume the path.

Mrs. Smith: What a correct and effective essay, although it was not long, I enjoyed it and I am proud to have such a student, I will consider a special grade for you.

Moon: Thank you, Mrs. Smith. Although I was stressed, but I was happy that my teacher liked my essay and encouraged me. These are the things that make me think more about my goals and want to achieve them

Sanaz: Moon, My friend? I'm talking to you.

Moon: Yes, what happened?

Sanaz: I was talking to you about Marmar.

Moon: Marmar?

Sanaz: Yes, look at her she's so nervous and upset.

Moon: Let's go and talk to her.

Sanaz: What are you saying? Again we have exam in next class with Mrs. Morian.

Moon: Yes, I know but you know that I cannot be indifferent to people's discomfort.

Sanaz: Yes, but good grade is not important for you?

Moon: Why is it important to me. But… But these are two different issues, let's go and heal with Marmar.

Sanaz: Oh no, class bell, let's go now. And I apologize for my behavior.

Moon: No problem. Oh, I'm stressed again I didn't study well.

Sanaz: I believe in you, you are smart and you will succeed in this exam like another exams else, so don't be afraid.

Moon: Everyone needs a friend like you to have hope.

Mrs. **Morian**: Hello, my smart girls.

Lily: Hello, how are you teacher? Did you have a good vacation?

Mrs. Morian: Thank you, lily. I am fine and I hope you will be ready for the exam.

Marmar: We are always ready for your exams.

Mrs. Morian: There is a problem?

Moon: No, teacher we talk about exam.

Mrs. Morian: Okay, here are the exam papers along with the answer sheet and your time is exactly one and a half hours.

Moon: Like always, I have a stress. But I have to control myself.

Lily: Moon, be calm. It's easy. Check it.

•*Transition: After an hour and a half*•

Mrs. Morian: Well, the exam time is over. I will collect the exam papers and tell you the mistakes after correcting them while you are free now and you can do whatever you like, just please quietly so that I can enter the grades.

Moon: Well, don't argue with me now. Tell me what time I will come to your house.

Sanaz: I said I will tell my mom and then I will let you know.

Moon: Okay, so I'll wait. Oh, I remembered that I was supposed to talk to you about changing my character.

Sanaz: Can you explain more?

Moon: I mean that I turned into a great and unique character.

Sanaz: Now I got it. We talk about it, okay?

Moon: It's great. And I was talking to Sanaz that whose Marmar said the class has been finished and we do not have any other classes.

Sanaz: No, are you sure?

Marmar: Yes.

Moon: Thank you for notifying us.

Sanaz: Well, Moon, I will see you on evening.

Moon: Sanaz?

Sanaz: Oh forgive me, I forgot. I'll see you in the evening.

Moon: No problem, my dear. We said goodbye and I started the way home. To be honest, the weather was a bit hot, but I can say that everything was enjoyable and it made me feel good. Finally, I reached home, opened the door, and went upstairs in my room.

Madusi: Hello, Moon.

Moon: Oh hi, my dear, I missed you. I thought you were with me.

Madusi: No, I was here and tried to work on your mother's mind.

Moon: My friend, you are wonderful.

Madusi: Go and message your friend.

Moon: Oh yes, you are right. But Madusi, I feel it's a bit strange that you read my mind.

Madusi: First call your friend. Then I will tell you about

Moon: Okay.

After that, I contacted Sanaz and told her that she came to our house. Madusi spoke about that discussion he promised.

Madusi: Do you know what's interesting? I thought that you were lying. But when I went to talk with my mother about Sanaz, she accepted without any question.

Madusi: You know over the time you trust me more.

Moon: I'm more enthusiastic every day that I understand more about you and the abilities you have.
Madusi: I knew that I chose the best person.

Moon: But now I have one question. My mother was able to see you in the future?

Madusi: This is a comprehensive question but I can say that you cannot see me now but in the future between yes or no.

Moon: Talking with Ali is very enjoyable, and I didn't understand the passage of time. As long as I hear the sound of door ring.

Sanaz: Hello Moon.

Moon: Oh, hi, but how are you?

Madusi: They act like they haven't seen each other for a long time.

Sanaz: But I think you were busy and I disturbed you.

Moon: No, don't think like that.

Sanaz: Now, I'm curious to know about these changes.

Moon: Wait, I will explain for you.

Sanaz: Explain it to me because I'm going crazy.

Moon: Okay, just promise that you can understand this story because when I told my mom, she was shocked.

Sanaz: You are saying the same thing yourself, so don't be surprised if I react.

Moon: Yes, you are right, now listen. Many months ago, before the new year new year, one night in the kitchen, I felt I could hear a voice, and I saw three little girls sitting there and they greeted me and introduced themselves.

Sanaz: Oh my God, how strange! I would have had a stroke if I were you.

Moon: I say that I was also shocked and couldn't believe it until they said that we are beings that came from the unseen world, we want to help you and we don't talk to anyone.

Sanaz: Was that the whole story? Didn't anything else happen?

Moon: It continues, just listen. One night, I called those three, but I didn't hear an answer.

Sanaz: No joke, I'm starting to get scared.

Moon: No, don't be afraid. After that I saw someone and he said my name is Madusi and I was surprised. I asked him who are you and he said I am Abraham.

Sanaz: Although first I was a little scared, this story is interesting. Now my question is, does the story continue?

Moon: Yes, and you may be even more shocked. And I talk about another family for two hours, and she really didn't know what to say.

Sanaz: I hope it's a joke because this doesn't make any sense. To be honest, I couldn't believe it at all and I can say that it took me a while to accept it. And you know it's very strange that the Earth has another version, whoever you tell them will think you're crazy.

Moon: Exactly, because when I told my mom about it, I thought I was rambling and she couldn't believe it. I feel that it has not yet reached that understanding and evolution.

Sanaz: I don't understand what you.

Moon: Madusi told me that it takes time to be able to understand. And in this way we will grow, understand and evolve in this story.

Sanaz: I am eager to see Madusi and talk to him.

Moon: But you can't see him or talk to him.

Sanaz: This was one of those tasteless jokes.

Moon: No, I'm serious. I even asked my mom once and she said that she doesn't see him, and when I told him, he replied that not all people can see me.

Sanaz: But when you think about the story, it is very interesting that beings from the unseen world communicate with you and try to help you, and after a while, they tell you that you have another family, that they are real, but they live in the second version of the earth, very strange. Shocking and interesting at the same time.

Moon: Well done, I agree with you, exactly what you are saying, even for myself, there are still many questions that Madusi should tell me about.

Sanaz: For example, what questions? About what?

CHAPTER FIVE

Moon: Well, about my family, what is their name, where do they live, what do they do, and maybe I can say hundreds of other questions related to this.

Sanaz: Oh God, you always have the same question about a general topic, what time is it?

Moon: Nine o'clock.

Sanaz: Oh, I have to go because I promised my mother that I will come back soon and help her with the housework.

Moon: Okay, no problem, just take care and I'll see you later.

Mother: Hi, my daughter.

Moon: Hi Mom, how are you?

Mother: I'm fine. Let's have dinner.

Moon: Wait, I will come now.

Mother: Okay, okay, I'm waiting.

Moon: Well, Madusi, let's go and have dinner.

Madusi: Again hello, let's go.

Moon: Madusi knew that I was messing with him and wanted to tease him so that we could laugh, that's why when we went down and had dinner, he looked like he's angry. After dinner, we went back to the room with Madusi and talked

Madusi: Well done, you said as Mrs. Smith said. You are very smart and quickly understand what happened.

Moon: Oh, but I think you were upset with me.

Madusi: Yes, I became upset because of what you said before dinner.

Moon: You are crazy and ridiculous. Well, I was joking with you so that we could laugh a little and change the atmosphere, but you became serious.

Madusi: Look at me. I don't mean not to joke, but you have to follow the rules.

Moon: I don't know but if I said something that upset you, I'm sorry.

Madusi: Are you apologizing to me?

Moon: Well, you said it yourself, I was upset.

Madusi: Oh, I'm kidding you too, I told myself to retaliate so that the story will be fun.

Moon: Ridiculous fool, you are very stupid.

Madusi: I don't understand at all why you are behaving like this; I was only joking.

Moon: But you shouldn't have made this joke because I show strange reactions to such behaviors.

Madusi: Let's talk about other things.

Moon: I think it's a very good idea. Please tell me, what have you been doing these past few days other than talking to me?

Madusi: Well, I'm telling the truth.

Moon: You should do the same because I hate lying and I really can't stand it.

Madusi: Okay, but I didn't want to lie. It was for fun.

Moon: I said I don't like this kind of behavior, but you continue, then you get upset when I tell you that your behavior is not right.

Madusi: I'm sorry. I won't repeat this behavior again, but let me tell you what I did.

Moon: I'm waiting.

Madusi: I went to our land and talked with the great masters about you.

Moon: Who are great and wise masters?

Madusi: Yes, we have a number of people in our land who are educated and have very high intelligence.

Moon: Wow, every day I find out more interesting things and it makes me more curious about the things I don't know.

Madusi: You are right, I know you may still be confused or even the things I tell you are unbelievable to you, but all this is true and I did not come to lie to you.

Moon: No, you got it wrong, I'm not saying that's what you mean, I'm just saying that it's very interesting and strange for me, and you know that it will take time for me to understand.

Madusi: It is definitely so and you have this opportunity, which means we will give you this permission.

Moon: Thank you, now tell me more about your masters. I'm eager to get to know them.

Madusi: Well, it's really great that you welcome us, it's very valuable for us.

Moon: Are you serious with me?

Madusi: Yes, I am honest with you, because before you, we wanted to connect other people to their real families, but they did not allow it themselves.

Moon: But why?

Madusi: Because they didn't trust us, they thought we wanted to hurt them, that's why such behavior made us, we leave and not try for them anymore.

Moon: I have a question. Do those people regret now?

Madusi: Don't know about them anymore and we don't know what happened for them.

Moon: But I think they will regret it later and maybe even now

Madusi: I agree with you, something like this definitely happened, but this regret is useless because they didn't wait, didn't trust, and many other things.

Moon: Well, you were explaining to me about the land masters.

Madusi: Oh, yes, I was forgetting, well, look, we have many masters in the land, if I want to explain it to you, it will take a long time, I will just briefly tell you the nicknames of some of them so that you understand.

Moon: Okay, no problem, but promise to explain to me in detail one day.

Madusi: It's hard, but I'll do my best.

Moon: I was joking. Go on.

Madusi: Master of light, wealth, blessing, salvation, peace, and many others.

Moon: How interesting and exciting! It reminded me of the historical stories I read.

Madusi: You are really patient, and trusting us is very valuable for us.

Moon: You are also very important to me and I am happy that you are here and we talk and talk about many things. I always needed someone like you.

Madusi: Are you kidding me?

Moon: No, Madusi, I am completely serious and I value you a lot, maybe at first bad things happened and I had a feeling of mistrust towards you, but now I really believe and I know that your words are not fake and you are telling the truth.

Madusi: You know, I got a really good feeling from your words and I'm sorry for a wrong judgment.

Moon: What are you talking about?

Madusi: Let me tell you so that you understand what I mean, after the previous experience and that family, when they explained to me about you, I was afraid and even started to judge and other things. And I'm really sorry.

Moon: It's okay. I myself may be judging many people. You definitely remember what I said and how I behaved on the first day when you introduced yourself.

Madusi: Yes, I remember, but now we have to let go and think about the future.

Moon: Yes you are right. Oh no. Oh no!

Madusi: What happened to you?

Moon: I forgot one important thing.

Madusi: Tell me. Maybe I can help you.

Moon: I have to make a PowerPoint about my favorite person in history. And why I like her.

Madusi: Who are you talking about?

Moon: Princess Diana.

Madusi: Turn on your laptop.

Moon: Every day I discover a new dimension of Madusi's personality.

Madusi: Your Power Point is ready and this is an explanatory summary.

Moon: Thank you so much, Madusi. Now I can sleep safely.

Madusi: I have to go. Our land because I have important things to do, so good night.

Moon: Tomorrow, I'll see you. I love the topics I discuss with Madusi and I enjoy talking with him and I was thinking about how strange things happen that change the equations.
Okay, sleeping is the best idea ever.

Madusi: Now it's morning and I talking to myself, I am an important part of the story of her evolution and growth, and this is very important to me.

Moon: Madusi?

Madusi: Yes?

Moon: What are you doing?

Madusi: Talking to myself.

Moon: One of my favorite things to do. Where's my mom?

Madusi: I don't know.

Moon: Mom? Mom?

Mother: Come into the warehouse.

Moon: What are you doing here?

Mother: You don't know?

Moon: Well, I understood.

Mother: Yes, it will take time but it will be fixed. What are you thinking about?

Moon: Well, I was thinking about how many months have passed since the first day I talked to Madusi.

Mother: Good. But let me advise you. It is true that he helps us, more you, but don't forget to try.

Moon: Yes, mom, I know this, I am trying my best and I see how much you are trying too, and I am really happy, but I know that everything will be alright.

Mother: Look, we have to try to fix the situation ourselves.

Moon: Yes, Mom, I said I know.

Mother: I think tomorrow you have an important exam.

Moon: Yes, math and science.

Mother: So, practice for it.

Madusi: She's right. Success does not come without effort. You must have to try to achieve what you want.

Moon: Yes, both of you are right. Days passed one after the other and my questions kept increasing and this made me not understand Mrs. Smith's lesson on Wednesday.

Sanaz: No problem, I explain for you.

Marmar: Girls?

Moon: Yes Marmar.

Marmar: I wanna say I you need help message me.

Moon: Thanks.

Sanaz: Tomorrow I will see you.

Moon: I said goodbye to Sanaz and headed home.

Madusi: Again, don't blame yourself.

Moon: But you know nothing.

Madusi: Thank you.

Moon: No, I mean Mrs. Smith classes are so important to me And she is my favorite teacher.

Madusi: Maybe we should talk less about it.

Moon: But my questions?

Madusi: I don't know what I can do.

Moon: Confusion is very annoying.

Madusi: I know.

Moon: Sometimes I'm very scared but I don't know why.

Madusi: Now just be relax. I promise to help you.

Moon: I had to listen to him, so I tried to be calm. I tried to enjoy what I saw in my around.

Madusi: Moon, it's 7 O'clock, wake up.

Moon: In morning? Oh, no. Oh no.

Madusi: Calm down.

Moon: I can't.

Madusi: I said calm down. It's 7 O'clock in Evening.

Moon: Really?? Thanks God.

Madusi: Yes, is not late. You know?

Moon: Sorry, I don't understand what's going on these days.

Madusi: We will fix it together.

Moon: After that sudden shock, I decided to read a few pages of my favorite book. And it was the best decision because after that I calmed down.

Madusi: Reading a book is a great hobby.

Moon: More than a just hobby. It has become a part of my life.

Madusi: Let's talk about your favorite books.

Moon: Fantasy books.

Madusi: Wow, what an interesting discussion. Explain it more.

Moon: And I explained a lot about my favorite fantasy books to my little friend.

Madusi: Do you like receiving gifts?

Moon: Of course, yes.

Madusi: So, I have a small gift for you but first close your eyes.

Moon: And?

Madusi: One of your favorite book series.

Moon: Wait, the folk of the air?

Madusi: Yes.

Moon: I have nothing to say. I have nothing to say and just I love you, Madusi.

Madusi: Again I wanna said your happiness is my happiness.

Moon: That day I didn't know what to do because I was so happy. But now I feel lost, I feel I need to find myself.

Madusi: I think you need a talk to someone.

Moon: Yes, but I don't know what to say.

Madusi: There's a no problem. Sometimes we have a problem with ourselves and it's a normal thing.

Moon: Yes, I agree with you but I am unpredictable. You must have realized that.

Madusi: I know, but this is not what we are talking about now.

Moon: I just wanted to mention it.

Madusi: It's a normal thing. I suggest you sleep, because your mind needs peace. I would love to stay and talk but I have to go to land because we have a ceremony.

Moon: You didn't tell me about it.

Madusi: The prayer ceremony that we call silence. Tomorrow I will explain for you, now good night.

Moon: Madusi always says things that make question in my mind about it. But not now, because it is better for me to sleep and let my mind rest a little.

Madusi: I am Madusi and I became your phone alarm.

Moon: Oh, you are so funny. What time is it?

Madusi: Don't worry you have time.

Moon: Yes, your idea, it was great.

Madusi: All of my ideas are great.

Moon: Selfish.

Madusi: No, I'm not selfish and I was just kidding.

Moon: I know. Well, I am ready now and let's go to school together today.

Madusi: Are you sure?

Moon: Is there any problem?

Madusi: No.

Moon: So, let's go. But promise me to stay calm.

Madusi: Okay, I'll try, but I can't promise.

CHAPTER SIX

Moon: He was really driving me crazy with his actions and behavior, but I love him because he's my best friend.

Madusi: Again to yourself?

Moon: About you.

Madusi: Tell me about it.

Moon: You know, I talk to myself about most of the people around me.

Madusi: Your features are interesting to me. Okay, continue it.

Moon: I like human relationships, but sometimes it makes me tired.

Madusi: Is this related to the issue of understanding and trust?

Moon: You are so smart. It includes part of the story. Sometimes I fear not being understood I know it's normal. But it bothers me.

Madusi: If you haven't forgotten, we talked about these issues before and I said that I will help you in this way.

Moon: No, I remember what you said. Finally, we arrived.

Marmar: Hey Moon.

Sanaz: Hi, good morning, my lovely.

Moon: Hi girls, what are doing?

Marmar: We were reviewing the lessons.

Moon: For exam? But I think today we don't have any exam.

Sanaz: Yes, today we don't have but tomorrow.

Moon: Oh, history exam.

Marmar: Hey my dear.

Sanaz: Did you see that man?

Moon: Yes, but who is he?

Sanaz: Our new teacher.

Moon: Is he a literature teacher.

Marmar: You are very smart.

Moon: I just guessed. It makes me feel good when people praise me. I went to class with my friends and I can say that today was one of the best classes I have ever experienced. Mr. Jones spoke very well and it was clear that he is very professional. And I like to socialize with other people.

Madusi: Proud of you.

Moon: Now we can talk until my friends come.

Madusi: They are coming

Moon: Oh, sorry, Madusi. We can talk on the way.

Madusi: What a great idea!

Moon: I also have good ideas. But wait you were supposed to explain to me about that ceremony.

Madusi: I will explain to you on the way.

Moon: Good.

Sanaz: Moon, we brought food for you too.

Moon: I love too.

Sanaz: We are a strong team.

Marmar: The best team.

Moon: This group must have a name.

Sanaz: Important point, yes.

Moon: Over time, we became closer with Maryam, and this was what made me happy. And if I want to be honest with myself, I can say that today was wonderful.

Madusi: I know it's because of me.

Moon: How much you love yourself.

Madusi: This is the right way.

Moon: Yes, but you are wrong.

Madusi: Just for fun.

Moon: I should have known you were joking.

Madusi: So you still don't know me completely.

Moon: 50-50, exactly like you.

Madusi: I accept it. But now let me explain to you about that ceremony.

Moon: Wait until we arrive, it's better than now.

Madusi: You are right.

Moon: So I can't wait to hear about.

Madusi: Yes, let's go up together.

Mother: Oh Moon.

Moon: Mommy, how are you?

Mother: I'm fine, and how are you?

Moon: Everything is fine. I can describe today as wonderful.

Mother: You made me happy.

Moon: The fact that you care about me is so valuable for me

Mother: It is true that sometimes we argue together, but I always care about you.

Moon: I love more than anyone.

Madusi: You make me jealous.

Moon: Be jealous.

Madusi: You finally understand my humor.

Moon: Historical moment between us.

Madusi: I feel successful.

Moon: You are so funny. Okay, Madusi, did you forget your promise?

Madusi: Of course no.

Moon: Well, I am waiting to hear you.

Madusi: We have many ceremonies in our land like glorify and praise ceremony.

Moon: Can you explain more?

Madusi: We pray for people in this ceremony and send them positive energy. The great masters are the head of this ceremony. You must write the information I give you.

Moon: Yes, I do it.

Madusi: Every day you proves more that you are looking for growth and development.

Moon: Yes, this is really what I am looking for, because is so important for me.

Madusi: Good, oh look at your phone.

Moon: Sanaz is calling.

Madusi: Answer her.

Moon: Sanaz called me via video call and said that she wanted to visit me today, but she couldn't and we started talking We can talk about a hundred different topics at the same time, after half an hour we said goodbye and I went downstairs because I heard my father voice.

Dad: Hi my girl.

Moon: Hello dad I missed you so much.

Dad: That's why I came and I wanna stay.

Mother: Stay? What are talking about?

Dad: I want to change my job.

Moon: I had a strange feeling.

Madusi: I have to stop arguing and fighting. Now is the time to focus on this.

Moon: While I was thinking that something bad might happen, I saw my parents talking quietly to each other.

Madusi: You can thank me.

Moon: Let me think, yes, I can do it.

Madusi: You are funnier than me.

Moon: I know.

Madusi: Selfish.

Moon: This is your characteristic, not mine.

Madusi: But I don't think so.

Moon: I am willing to bet with you.

Madusi: I surrender, you are right.

Moon: I am always right.

Madusi: I am proud of myself when I do something useful.

Moon: I really like to hear the voice of your mind.

Madusi: But sorry you can't.

Moon: I know but I sometimes I wish I had magic powers.

Madusi: Becoming invisible? Or reading people's minds.

Moon: Maybe both?

Madusi: Having power has two sides good and bad. And it depends on you what you want to use it for.

Moon: Tell me about your powers.

Madusi: But it's a long story.

Moon: We can talk about it one day. What do you think?

Madusi: Yes, yes. We passed the previous months and now we are here.

Mother: We must learn from bad and difficult moments in our life.

Moon: I don't want to learn anything.

Mother: Don't be stubborn.

Moon: Sometimes it is necessary.

Dad: Everything is good??

Mother: I don't know.

Dad: Look at me. I promise we will fix everything, but together.

Moon: I need solitude and peace.

Mother: Let's go and leave her alone.

Madusi: My friend let's talk together. See, loss is part of our life. I know, understanding the situation and realizing is not easy.

Moon: I think you are right, but it is difficult.

Madusi: This is what I am talking about, that changes and hardships are painful.

Moon: I don't want another family, I want to be at peace on this earth with my current family.

Madusi: So, the future is not important to you?

Moon: Yes, no, I don't know anything right you. I miss our previous house and my room. How happy we were, Christmas and New Year decorations.

Madusi: You forgot something.

Moon: Oh yes, my school and friends. If I went to a new school, I would be very upset.

Madusi: Maybe what I'm saying is wrong, but try to see the positive and good things even in bad situations.

Moon: I agree with you and this is an important point. Just now I was thinking that helping can be spiritual and psychological. It is not always necessary for people to do something for us.

Madusi: Your thoughts are change in the right direction.

Moon: Do you think this is true?

Madusi: Not always, but changing wrong thoughts yes.

Moon: Why not always?

Madusi: Because sometimes you may change yourself because you want to be liked by other people. I think you should be yourself.

Moon: He knows very well how to change the subject. Yes, and I try to be myself because I find it more lovable.

Madusi: This is exactly what we should all do.

Moon: Yes. Do you want coffee?

Madusi: Actually, I don't know.

Moon: You don't know?

Madusi: I'm kidding.

Moon: I know you better than yourself.

Madusi: I don't like to say it, but I agree.

Moon: Don't forget that I am stubborn.

Madusi: No, please no.

Moon: We are slowly understanding each other better.

Madusi: Are you talking about my reaction?

Moon: Yes because It is related to the understanding my humor.

Madusi: Oh, yes.

Moon: I went to the kitchen and saw my mother making tea.

Mother: Tea?

Moon: Oh no, Mom. I need coffee.

Mother: I have a little work outside.

Moon: With my friends' moms?

Mother: Yes, Sepi and Soraya.

Moon: Have a nice day, Mom.

Mother: Mutual feeling. I'll see you when I come back.

Moon: Okay, Mom.

Nahid: After a long time, I decided to have a friendly gathering. Talking to these two beautiful ladies through my daughter is very precious to me.

Soraya: Hi, first member of Women's Club.

Nahid: Hello Soraya. Where's Sepi?

Soraya: It will arrive in five minutes. Now let's talk together. At the same time, we can see what's going on at home.

Madusi: I love your coffees delicious than Mommy Nafise.

Moon: Treat with respect.

Madusi: So I have to be respectful.

Moon: In everywhere on this Earth or second Earth.

Madusi: I promise, you were supposed to talk with me about the dream you had seen.

Moon: Yes, in my dream, I saw some people whose faces were not clear, but I felt they were familiar to me.

Madusi: Mommy Nafise and Father Reza.

Moon: My second Earth grandparents. Right?

Madusi: Yes, this is a very good thing about you and them.

Moon: Can you explain more?

Madusi: Of course, look, when you meet them in your dream, it will be easier for you to understand this matter in reality.

Moon: You are right, but, at first I felt scared, but then not, is this normal?

Madusi: Yes, it is normal because you are getting to know a new dimension of life and your surroundings. But you should wait for one important fundamental change.

Moon: What are you talking about?

Madusi: You have to wait until that day and I will be with you in this way and I will help you to understand it.

Moon: It gave me a strange feeling.

Madusi: I say again that these things are normal and don't be afraid.

Moon: I will try.

Madusi: Good, now let's drink our coffee. It's almost eight o'clock, so let's go see what's going on in the city and this is about women's club.

Nahid: Are you kidding me?

Sepideh: No she's right.

Nahid: because it's shockable.

Soraya: We were surprised when we found out.

Sepideh: Big thanks to our girls.

Nahid: By the way, we were talking about this before you came.

Sepideh: Wow! My opinion is that we should have women's club three days a week.

Soraya: Fantastic, I agree with you.

Nahid: We can't talk about many things, visit different places in the city.

Madusi: I was also watching Moon Mother and her friends from a distance and it gave me an interesting feeling and I thought that both of them are in the stage of evolution and growth. And at this moment, I teleported myself back home and said hello again.

Moon: Where were you? I was talking when I saw you were not there.

Madusi: Sorry, I had to go and check something.

Mood: No problem I forgive you.

Madusi: You make me ashamed.

Mood: Am I kidding you?

Madusi: I am also serious.

Moon: It is in your best interests to be serious at times.

CHAPTER SEVEN

Madusi: I know, my dear Moon.

Moon: Good, was it the doorbell?

Madusi: Must be your mother.

Moon: Yes. I went and opened the door in front of my mother and she hugged me.

Mother: You are very precious to me and this is for you.

Moon: Mom, I love you too, but what is this?

Mother: A gift for you because I wanted to thank you for introducing me to a lovely group.

Moon: Oh yes, I understand what you mean now. I became happy.

Madusi: Thinking about them is both difficult and easy, as if they are really living and next to them, you will notice all aspects of life.

Moon: I realized that you are talking to yourself.

Madusi: About your family.

Moon: If you like, we can talk about it.

Madusi: I am eager.

Moon: So, let's go up and talk. As much as Madusi is interesting to me, it seems that I am also interesting to him.

Madusi: I want to protest you.

Moon: But why?

Madusi: Because you talk to yourself?

Moon: Are you kidding me or are you serious?

Madusi: I am not joking.

Moon: Well, I know you're joking.

Madusi: You are smarter than I think.

Moon: It makes me happy that you think like this.

Madusi: Let's talk about it.

Moon: About what?

Madusi: You are not smart.

Moon: What?

Madusi: Sorry, it's for fun.

Moon: I forgive you this time too. Okay, you said that all aspects of our personality are interesting for you.

Madusi: Because you behave both badly and well, of course, this is normal, but sometimes you confuse me.

Moon: These feelings and behavior between us is normal and you definitely understand that but I think it depends on the situation, you know?

Madusi: But in my opinion, controlling anger and excitement is also important.

Moon: Of course, yes, especially controlling anger. Sometimes I can't control it, but not always.

Madusi: What you said has many deep and meaningful points.

Moon: I have a one question. What is a tunnel?

You talked about it many times, but you didn't say what is tunnel.

Madusi: The teleport tunnel is like a communication way to connect the worlds together.

Moon: Wow, how exciting! Can I also go into the tunnel?

Madusi: Yes, but not now.

Moon: Why? I have passion for many things but you are stopping me.

Madusi: I am not an obstacle. I'm just saying it's not time yet.

Moon: I don't know how to react.

Madusi: I told you before that you should be patient.

Moon: I am usually a patient person, but sometimes I get tired.

Madusi: I think you are referring to something else.

Moon: You think right.

Madusi: No problem, I can do something for you, but then you have to promise not to talk about it too much until the time comes.

Moon: I promise you.

Madusi: Look at it, it looks like a simple ring, but this is my secret tool. And now I will tell you what I mean.

Moon: Of course, it is not so simple and it looks very beautiful.

Madusi: Okay, now what I want to show you is important then. Look at that screen.

Moon: I can't believe it. They are my family. I am also present there.

Madusi: I understand that you are shocked but I had to do it because I had to prove things to you.

Moon: No, I am also happy that you did it, now I have strange feelings. And my mind is filled with new questions.

Madusi: You are not the first and you will not be the last.

Moon: What do you mean?

Madusi: I already said that you are not the first person I talked to about the real family and you are not the last.

Moon: Wait, you mean you might leave me and go to someone else?

Madusi: No, because I am your Abraham and I will help you to a better life and knowledge.

Moon: Progress, learning, and growth are not easy.

Madusi: I agree and disagree with what you said because as you know. it is also about strong will. You can't sit and tell yourself that everything will be fine one day. Life is not a joke. It is hard and difficult, but there are also easy days and happy days.

Moon: You speak very deeply and beautifully and also effectively.

Madusi: Thank you. I was talking about life and that for a good mood, you have to strive for success, you have to continue, and that failure and disappointment are part of your path.

Moon: Do you think I can change?

Madusi: Yes, it is true that you still have some wrong thoughts, but you have improved a lot compared to the first days.

Moon: So I can be proud of myself.

Madusi: More than anytime. And we entered to one of the most important moments of life. It means late adolescence.

Sanaz: I know I'm going to miss you.

Moon: Don't be dramatic; we are not going to break up together.

Sanaz: But the best memories of these years were with you two.

Moon: I think you did not understand what I said.

Sanaz: Yes, but admit that there is a strange feeling going on.

Marmar: I agree with both of you.

Moon: No, you can't.

Marmar: I know you are kidding.

Moon: You know me well. Girls, I brought you a souvenir.

Sanaz: You are the sweetest and loveliest.

Moon: Letters I wrote and sealed for you two.

Sanaz: You know my interests very well.

Marmar: Letters is one of my favorite things.

Moon: Besties' mentality.

Sanaz: The best trio in the world.

Marmar: Friendships that start from hate each other are very interesting.

Moon: The past has no value.

Sanaz: No, it's very important.

Moon: I talk about our acquaintance.

Sanaz: Okay, I got it. My bad.

Moon: No problem.

Marmar: I wanna hug you two and I want to say that I will see you two again.

Sanaz: And I want to say that I will see you again.

Moon: After the emotional talk, I said goodbye to my friend and I went home and started writing as always.

Madusi: Hello, Moon.

Moon: Welcome back my little friend. You were gone for a week and I missed you.

Madusi: But now I am here and we are going to talk about many things together again. What are doing?

Moon: I am more eager than ever. I'm writing.

Madusi: About what?

Moon: Like always about everything.

Madusi: I really want to read it.

Moon: This is the fifth notebook. You know?

Madusi: Yes, because I was always by your side.

Moon: It is precious to me.

Madusi: Many years have passed since the first time we talked to you.

Moon: I got emotional.

Madusi: Me too. We have many memories together. We spent good and bad days together.

Mother: Moon?

Moon: Yes Mommy?

Mother: Sanaz is here.

Moon: But? I can't believe it.

Sanaz: Surprise.

Moon: I hate you and I love you at the same time.

Sanaz: We have mutual feelings.

Moon: But you made me happy.

Sanaz: So I succeeded.

Moon: Yes Sanaz

Sanaz: Please no.

Moon: I'm kidding.

Sanaz: Anyway, I have a one gift for and I know you will be happy.

Moon: A gift for me?

Sanaz: After saying goodbye to you, we went to the store with Marmar.

Moon: But you two tried to make me emotional.

Sanaz: We were bothering you.

Moon: I hate you.

Sanaz: When I tease you, it means you are my favorite person.

Moon: I know this because it's a fact. Anyway, give me my gift.

Sanaz: Here you are.

Moon: A box?

Sanaz: I said that you will be surprised.

Moon: What? Oh God, I love you, Sanaz. I love you. One of the best gifts I got in my life.

Sanaz: We knew you loved Taylor Swift. That's why we decided to buy your favorite albums.

Moon: I was very happy to see Sanaz again, and most importantly, the gift she gave me is very valuable to me.

Sanaz: I love your new room.

Moon: It's all about my favorite.

Sanaz: More than favorite, sometimes I wish I was a teenager in NYC in 80s.

Moon: My eternal wish

Sanaz: Yes now also we are in New York but that time is unforgettable for who lives.

Moon: I have one idea. Before, I told you, about Madusi magic wand.

Sanaz: You have a unique mind. But what you say is possible?

Moon: My mother is not at home now and she said she will be back in three hours. Now, wait, Madusi? My friend?

Madusi: Yes, Moon?

Moon: I explained the story to Madusi and asked him to do what we want for us.

Madusi: I can do it, but there is a condition that you don't talk about it with anyone right now.

Moon: We promise and we don't talk about it to anyone.

Madusi: Okay, hold each other's hands. Close your eyes and be ready.

Moon: At this moment, I felt changes and heard the voices of different people. I think now we can open our eyes.

Madusi: Yes, welcome To NYC in 1985.

Sanaz: The most incredible moment of my life.

Moon: Madusi, we love you.

Sanaz: It's true that I don't see your friend, but I understand his effects.

Moon: This is great. Oh what is this?

Madusi: Open it and use it.

Moon: A vintage camera.

Sanaz: So beautiful and now we can take a picture from anything we can see here. I am unique and lovable.

Sanaz: So beautiful and now we can take a picture from anything we can see here.

Moon: Fantastic idea. But Madusi, when we talk to another's they can believe our words?

Madusi: Between yes or no, but I try to make them believe your words.

Moon: Thank you. Sanaz, let's go and enjoy together.
But really I need a coffee.

Sanaz: Good news, we are next to the coffee shop.

Moon: Oh my heart, the Beatles.

Sanaz: One of my favorite bands ever.

Moon: I still couldn't believe that we are in the 80s and we are taking pictures of everything around us with Polaroid camera.

Sanaz: Everything looks so beautiful and dreamy.

Moon: Now we are experiencing things that we love.

Sanaz: You should be thankful for having them in your life.

Madusi: She's right; I am unique and lovable.

Moon: Madusi said he's so lovely.

Sanaz: Oh, cute boy.

Moon: You mean selfish?

Sanaz: No, I agree with him.

Moon: I understand what you mean.

Sanaz: Yes. Now we can go walk in the city.

Moon: and taking pictures or listening to music from famous bands.

Sanaz: Let's go, Moon and Madusi.

Moon: I love you, my dear.

Sanaz: My too. Oh, look at that poster.

CHAPTER EIGHT

Moon: Which one?

Sanaz: That one, the Beatles members.

Moon: I saw it now.

Sanaz: The Smiths or The Beatles?

Moon: Your question is like saying do you like your mother or your father more.

Sanaz: I got the answer.

Moon: What is your opinion about them?

Sanaz: I made a mistake, sorry.

Moon: Sorry if I upset you.

Sanaz: No, everything is okay.

Moon: Good, how beautiful everything is!

Sanaz: Moon, loot at that car again I have a one idea.

Moon: I know what you want to say. I agree with you, so let's do it.

Sanaz: What an interesting power!

Moon: Sanaz and I went to the man who I think was the owner of the cars.

Sanaz: Hi.

Mr. Bono: Hello, ladies. How can I help you?

Moon: Are these cars only for sale?

Mr. Bono: My cars are for rent and for sale.

Sanaz: So we can rent one of these cars?

Moon: Finally, we rented a car and drove around the city, what an unforgettable and enjoyable experience.

Sanaz: Don't talk to yourself at this moment, talk to me.

Moon: Okay. Oh, be careful.

Sanaz: My driving is low risk.

Moon: I know. Let me call Madusi.

Madusi: Again hello, Moon. What are you doing?

Moon: It is not clear? We rented a car and we are having fun.

Madusi: What a wonderful experience. But I have to tell you that time is running out.

Moon: Yes we know.

Madusi: Good.

Moon: We returned to Mr. Bono and thanked him.

Mr. Bono: I hope your experience with my car was enjoyable.

Sanaz: It was more than good.

Moon: We said goodbye to Mr. Bono and went to a lonely alley, held each other's hands, and returned home.

Madusi: Open your eyes.

Sanaz: How different everything was.

Moon: And beautiful.

Sanaz: You know you know we have to find good things from the ugliest things and the worst moment in our life but 70s to 80s are my favorite decades.

Madusi: They are talking to each other and I say to myself, I wish I could talk to the people around the moon. I was talking to myself about my thoughts when the moon called me.

Moon: Everything is Okay, Madusi?

Madusi: Yes, I don't know.

Moon: Why my friend?

Madusi: I don't know, sometimes I want to talk to other people around you.

Moon: No, you can't.

Madusi: I know.

Moon: Please don't be upset, my friend.

Madusi: I also ruminate like you.

Moon: Rumination is very annoying, try to get better.

Madusi: Your advice is also very informative.

Moon: I learned from you. Oh, I'm so sleepy.

Madusi: Sleep is the best thing in the world.

Moon: In any situation, I choose sleep.

Madusi: We talk together later.

Moon: Good night.

•*As time goes on, we get closer to the critical moments.* •

Madusi: I don't know; let me check.

Moon: Oh God! Oh no!

Madusi: What happened to you? Everything is okay?

Moon: I said no.

Madusi: Be calm and explain it.

Moon: I can't because today is my soul mate's birthday and I did nothing.

Madusi: Listen to me, be calm and call Marmar.

Moon: Yes, you are right. Where's my phone?

Madusi: Here you are.

Moon: Thanks. After this call, please give me that relaxation potion.

Madusi: Okay. I clearly saw how much she cares about the people around her. And the thing that attracts my attention is the mutual feelings between them. I feel that they know boundaries very well.

Moon: Madusi, come down. We must go shopping together.

Madusi: Just me and you?

Moon: No, Marmar is coming. I'm going to get ready. Let me know when she calls.

Madusi: At the same time, I decided to be curious, that's why I went to Sanaz house.

Sanaz: Mami, I said I don't like this dress, oh God, I can't live with you here we difference of opinion.

Simon: Sis, tonight is your birthday fight together after tonight's party.

Soraya: Enough, try to be worthy, my loves.

Sanaz: Sorry, Mami.

Madusi: How unpredictable everything is between them. It's time to go back, thank God that Marmar has not called yet.

Moon: Where are you?

Madusi: I'm here. Look up.

Moon: Oh, my phone. I think Marmar has arrived. Let's go.

Madusi: The stories that happen between them are very interesting, strange and endearing to me.

Marmar: Hello after a month.

Moon: But we had a video call together yesterday.

Marmar: That is not real.

Moon: It's true. We better go to the store because it might be late.

Marmar: Yes, yes. Put things on the back seat.

Madusi: I am happy when I see that she has formed a deep friendship with Maryam.

Moon: Let me say something. Again thanks for that gift. Honestly, it made me very happy and I still feel good.

Marmar: You are my valuable friend and I love you more than you think.

Moon: Same mood about you and Sanaz.

Marmar: Powerful trio. I think we arrived. Go in and I will come.

Madusi: Moon. What do you want to buy for her?

Moon: You will understand. Marmar also came.

Madusi: I have to say again how much they care about everything and everyone around them. They understood mutual respect very well.

Moon: Let me help you.

Marmar: No Thanks
Let's go because we have so many works.

Moon: Birthday party starts at eight, right?

Marmar: Yes, we have time but we have to plan properly.

Moon: You know this very well.

Marmar: Sweetie. Well, let's go to our house and do our works and surprises.

Moon: I like this kind of celebrations because I feel good.

Madusi: But it is better to say that you also like all the celebrations of different countries.

Moon: My friend, how are you?

Madusi: I'm fine. Is everything going well?

Moon: And yes, you are right, I love anything that makes me happy.

Madusi: I like your thoughts.

Moon: And you know I praise simple pleasures; they are our last refuge.

Madusi: You can be a role model.

Moon: Role model? No, I can't.

Madusi: You can, believe in yourself.

Moon: We can talk about this later, now we have a lot of work.

Madusi: So, I will go to our land because we have a ceremony.

Moon: After my friend left, Marmar and I started making gifts.

Marmar: Finally. I am very tired, but now I have to go and get ready, so I will back.

Moon. Little friend, are you back?

Madusi: Yes, I'm back. Do you have any work with me?

Moon: No, I just wanted call you.

CHAPTER NINE

Madusi: What a beautiful box!

Moon: We made it together and I think Sanaz will like it or I don't know.

Madusi: Don't ignore me.

Moon: What do you mean?

Madusi: I am talking about gifts.

Moon: I understand now. We also bought comic and books for here.

Madusi: So. Her favorite genre is superhero.

Moon: One of her favorite genres.

Madusi: I went to your friend's house.

Moon: Always as I said, you are so funny.

Madusi: But I'm not kidding because I was there.

Moon: Believable and unbelievable.

Marmar: Moon, are you ready?

Moon: Write the things we want to talk about in the notebook.

Madusi: This is an important point.

Moon: Marmar told me to drive and I liked her idea, so I did it and finally we arrived.

Marmar: Did you tell your mother to go to our house?

Moon: Yes, I told her and she said okay.

Marmar: Good, because I was worried about it.

Moon: No, don't worry. After that, she told me something that shocked me.

Marmar: I really do it.

Moon: Sometimes you are very unpredictable.

Marmar: Like football?

Moon: Yes, exactly like football.

Madusi: While I was listening to their conversations, I decided to go and see what Sanaz's reaction is.

Sanaz: No, I can't believe it. Mommy you are kidding me I know.

Soraya: I don't. Marmar texted me and she said sorry. You want me to show you that massage?

Madusi: It was a strange scene, but I had seen it before, because their love language is annoying. But, I immediately went outside to see what Marmar and Moon are doing.

Soraya: Girls, enter through the secret door of the house.

Moon: Okay, we are aware.

Marmar: Try to be calm.

Moon: Finally, we entered through the secret door and luckily, Sanaz had not noticed our presence yet.

Madusi: How intelligent and mysterious they are!

Moon: I am very similar to you, my friend. We saw Sanaz doing preparations and we said hello to her.

Sanaz: What? I can't believe it, you two here?

Marmar: Surprise! We are the best friends in the world you forget it?

Moon: This was Maryam's plan, but I helped her.

Sanaz: I wanna HUG you two.

Moon: Let's start the party.

Marmar: Aunt Soraya, join us.

Artemis: Hi everyone. I am a special surprise.

Sanaz: Wait What? I can't believe it. Artemis is here?

Moon: Yes Sanaz. Welcome back Artemis. I've missed you more than you think.

Marmar: Sanaz always talks about you.

Artemis: You know, I'm so happy because I came back on my little sister's birthday.

Soraya: Shall we not start the celebration?

Artemis: Yes, Mommy, let's be happy tonight.

Simon: Hey, fam look at the camera.

Artemis: What a beautiful photo! Print them for me too. I want the memory of tonight to be with me when I return to London.

Moon: Don't talk about it now.

Artemis: Yes, you are right.

Sanaz: Besties, we haven't taken a picture together yet.

Marmar: Simon, take a picture of us.

Simon: Did you hire a photographer? You know I'm kidding.

Moon: Tonight was one of the best and unforgettable experiences of my life, and after we gave the gifts, good feelings flowed and Sanaz's reaction made us happy.

Sanaz: My lovely Pookies.

Moon: I love your vocabulary.

Marmar: You always surprise us.

Sanaz: You should be happy to have me in your life.

Moon: Yes, we are happy.

Artemis: Everyone listen to me. Cheers to more unforgettable memories together. Cheers to more fun together.

Moon: I can't forget tonight.

Marmar: I also agree with you.

Sanaz: I have a suggestion.
Girls' night. We can watch a movie, talk about it together, and do other things.

Moon: Sanaz decided us to have a girls' night. And this is what I needed.

Marmar: Power TRIO.

Simon: power trio? Are you kidding?

Sanaz: Tonight No but after that I have for you wait.

Simon: No, I'm joking.

Moon: You underestimated us.

Simon: I said sorry.

Sanaz: Now we laugh at you. Let's go, girls.

Moon: When I am with them, I feel like we are a family.

Madusi: You are right, because they are your family.

Moon: I missed you, my smart little friend.

Madusi: I was also at the party and I had a great time.

Moon: Madusi, can you show me what my mother is doing now?

Madusi: We have little time, no problem. Like last time, close your eyes.

Moon: I closed my eyes and opened them after Madusi said, 'What a strange and interesting thing happened.'

Madusi: You see them but they cannot see you.

Moon: Because we became invisible.

Madusi: Yes, but don't forget that we have to go back when the timer rings.

Moon: I am attentive. At that moment, I was listening to their conversation and I was happy that my mother's mental state has improved.

Mehrafarin: Don't call me mother.

Nahid: Oh God, I love you so much. You look like a Soraya's sister.

Maisen: Sometimes they argue about it.

Nahid: I know and they are so funny.

Iris: It even tells us to be cautious.

Mehrafarin: It's good that I'm here too.

Iris: You know we are joking.

Mehrafarin: Yes, I know, and that's why I came back.

Maison: So, you are going to live with us.

Iris: Do I understand correctly?

Mehrafarin: I knew you would be surprised.

Maison: I feel happy.

Nahid: Even I liked your personality, dignity, and passion.

Mehrafarin: Your feelings are mutual.

Madusi: Moon, it's time to go back.

Moon: Oh yes, you are right, let's go back to Aunt Soraya's.

Madusi: Well, we are back successfully.

Moon: Successfully? What do you mean?

Madusi: You know that sometimes the equations may get messed up and it becomes impossible to return.

Moon: I feel scared. Maybe it's better not to travel in time together anymore.

Madusi: You don't understand what I mean, I'm saying this happens to someone who can't come back the first time, not to you who have successfully done it several times.

Moon: Now I understand exactly what you mean. I will answer my mother and then we will talk again

Madusi: Moon has a very interesting and unique personality and her friends are like this, that is, I feel that she is in contact with people whose personality type as close to her own.

Moon: Madusi? Where are you?

Madusi: I was talking to myself about you.

Moon: Do you want to talk about it?

Madusi: I spoke about your personality many times and of course you have changed a lot in these years but there are things about you that have not changed much.

Moon: At the same moment that I wanted to talk to Madusi, Marmar, and Sanaz entered the room.

Sanaz: But I'm sad that you didn't come.

Moon: I don't know what happened, but I got a headache and I preferred to wait for you two.

Marmar: But tomorrow we will definitely go out together.

Moon: And you two will come to our house tomorrow night. I talked to my mother and she agreed.

Marmar: I have a good feeling that your condition is getting better.

Moon: There is still a long way to go to improve the situation, but I also feel good.

Sanaz: Yes we know. Don't forget that we are with you.

Moon: It is very valuable for me to have you two by my side.

Marmar: Let me hug you.

Moon: After hugging, we were thinking about the series.

Sanaz: Let me check what I have here.

Marmar: I love that pink *Floyd* vinyl.

Moon: *Wish You Were Here* and *The Dark Side of the Moon*. Second Album is my favorite.

Marmar: Yes, I know because I love this album too.

Sanaz: Please pay attention to me.

Moon: Did you find the desired series?

Sanaz: Yes, don't underestimate me. Let's watch *HIMYM* together.

Marmar: The best idea in the world is watching sitcoms together.

Sanaz: Random?

Moon: I think you, Marmar, what's your opinion?

CHAPTER TEN

Marmar: I agree with you two. Let's watch one or two episodes randomly.

Moon: I feel like I'm in the cinema.

Marmar: I also wanted to say this.

Moon: Really? Besties mentality again.

Sanaz: Hey you two don't forget me.

Marmar: No, because you have a special place in our hearts.

Sanaz: I just wanted to joke.

Marmar: Funniest person I've seen.

Moon: You are right, because Sanaz is even funnier than me.

Sanaz: We can talk later, now it's time to watch the series.

Moon: So, play it.

Madusi: Their favorite things are very attractive to me like movies, books and especially music. Sometimes I feel as if they don't belong to this decade or century.

Moon: I love Barney and Robin's relationship but I identify with Ted.

Marmar: Wait what? I can't believe it this is historical moment.

Moon: You know better, I may not like a person or a character but after a while I get attracted to it.

Sanaz: You are a very interesting person around me but we are so happy because you like Ted's character now.

Madusi: Everything they do is real and without stereotypes, the things they say, the things they do I choose the right person for communication. And through her I met other good people. Oh, like it's time to go back to the land because something seems to have happened.

Moon: Madusi communicated with me through my mind and told me he was going to their land. It was one of the few times he spoke to me like this.

Marmar: Moon? Everything is okay?

Moons: Yes, everything is great and good.

Marmar: Good. Sanaz said coffee or tea?

Moon: Now I want coffee.

Sanaz: Okay, my friend.

Marmar: I feel like I'm addicted to coffee.

Moon: Jade West once said: I love coffee. Yeah, I know a lot of people say they love coffee but they just mean that they like it a lot. I LOVE it. Like sometimes I swear I wanna marry coffee.

Marmar: The thing you always talk about BUT I think I became like the Gilmores.

Moon: And you know that I love Rory and I hate at the same time.

Marmar: And exactly i know your reasons.

Sanaz: I am back. Here you are, your coffees. What are you talking about?

Moon: Spanish latte is love of my life. We talk about characters.

Sanaz: But wait, you said who's your love of your life?

Marmar: The best question.

Moon: Do not put me in such a situation.

Sanaz: Don't forget that fact.

Moon: Do you think I'm a clown?

Marmar: Sometimes.

Moon: Oh God! Shame on you.

Marmar: You know very well that I know your humor.

Moon: And this is my mistake.

Marmar: Wait, are you serious?

Moon: Yes, I'm serious.

Marmar: This is incredible.

Sanaz: Look at her. She is laughing. It is clear that she is joking.

Moon: You were fooled.

Marmar: I hate you two more than you think.

Moon: Let me think about it.

Marmar: About what?

Moon: About what you are saying.

Sanaz: Girls, enough. Let's be relaxed. And drink coffee.

Moon: We are interesting people, you know why?

Şanaz: Because it is time to sleep and we are drinking coffee.

Marmar: Good point.

Moon: Yes, but no problem. I have a solution. At this moment, I called Madusi and asked him to do something so that we can sleep comfortably.

Madusi: Sometimes I feel like they are crazy because they say strange things and behave humorously. But it doesn't matter, I have to discover new things about them.

Moon: I was immersed in my dreams and at that moment I woke up when I heard Sanaz's scream, and I quickly went to see what happened.

Marmar: I know you are excited but keep calm.

Sanaz: I can't be calm, I can't.

Moon: Can you tell me what happened because I was scared.

Marmar: Excited scream.

Moon: What the hell is going on here? Please explain in clearly way because I don't understand anything.

Marmar: Do you remember that brand and modeling?

Moon: Yes, did they accept you?

Sanaz: Yes and I am very happy because I feel that I am getting closer to my dreams.

Marmar: We are so happy for you, sweetheart.

Moon: We must celebrate together. Your success is our success.

Marmar: Moon is right. I have an idea.

Sanaz: You two are my biggest supporters. Tell us your idea?

Marmar: Tomorrow we can go and watch the NHL.

Sanaz: It's true that I'm a New York Rangers fan, but I know. We're going to have a good day.

Moon: I can still compete with you.

Sanaz: Of course, New York Rangers is better than New York Islanders.

Moon: Are you sure? Let's talk about it with fact.

Marmar: We will discuss later. Now we have to go and buy tickets.

Moon: We can do this online.

Sanaz: Artemis said she wanted to talk to me. I'll be back soon. I didn't know exactly what she wanted to talk to you about, but I could guess.

Artemis: We have to talk about many things together.

Sanaz: What do you mean, sis?

Artemis: You know that you are going to know another dimension and experience many things and as an older sister, I have to talk to you about it.

Sanaz: She talked about important and interesting things and I'm really happy to have her in my life because her words and advices have always helped me.

Artemis: You are very precious to me, my little sister.

Sanaz: Hey, I'm not the younger sister anymore because I turned 20.

Artemis: You will always be my little sister and Simon will always be my little brother.

Sanaz: I think they want to tell me something.

Moon: Hi Artemis, how are you, girl?

Artemis: I'm fine. We were talking in this nice weather.

Moon: Weather is amazing. I love it. But this is not important now because I want to say that we managed to buy tickets.

Artemis: Tickets? What are you talking about?

Sanaz: National Hockey League.

Artemis: Oh yes NHL. Maybe you changed your team.

Sanaz: You forgot? They are fans of New York Islanders.

Artemis: Oh, I had forgotten.

Moon: I have to inform my mother.

Marmar: Aren't we supposed to come to your house, so tell her right there.

Moon: You mentioned an important point.

Sanaz: Wait for me when I come back.

Moon: After half an hour and saying goodbye to Artemis, we went home with my friend. I want to be honest, I missed my mother, that's why I hugged her.

Mother: I missed you so much, my girl. Come in, my girls, and go to moon room. Thank you, Aunt Nahid.

Moon: After my friend went to my room, I talked to my mother about tomorrow and the ticket and she said that there is no problem. But MOM, I can't believe it, because even though you changed, I felt that you would disagree.

Mother: I may still disagree with many things and behaviors, but I try to think about them and see if I'm really doing it right.

Moon: You are the best mother in the world. Did father send a letter?

Mother: Yes, and he said he would be back soon and it stays here.

Moon: This is the best news in the world because I miss him so much. I felt very good after hearing the news, after that I joined my friends and we talked till night

Sanaz: We don't not judge anyone, also us.

Marmar: We are much funnier than anyone can think.

Sanaz: This is our characteristic. Oh, look at *Pinterest* homepage.

Marmar: Matthew from *Criminal Minds*, right?

Sanaz: Wait a second, continue the series and don't bore me.

Marmar: I promise you that I will do it especially because of Matthew.

Moon: He is one of my favorite actors.

Marmar: A question has been bothering me. Who is your favorite singer that you like the most?

Moon: I and Lana have so much in common. We're both obsessed with ELVIS.

Marmar: Okay, I got it the answer. And it didn't surprise me too much. I saw how much you like him and his music.

Moon: He made me love the guitar, you know. Sometimes I wish he were still alive.

Marmar: I feel that songs, movies and even old people are more beautiful and real.

Sanaz: I think now is the time to tell her about that experience.

Moon: Oh yes, you are right I also feel that we must say.

Madusi: I agree with your friend and there is no obstacle to say it.

Moon: Now we can safely talk about it. One day, I and Sanaz traveled in time.

Marmar: Travel in time? I don't understand anything from your words.

Moon: This interest in the past is common between us when Sanaz came to our house and we talked about many things, I thought that I asked Madusi to take us to the 80s.

Sanaz: And he even gave Moon an old camera to capture all the details.

Marmar: I got confused. At the same time, I understand what you are saying and I don't.

Moon: Let me show you the camera and the photos.

Sanaz: Maybe if I were you, it would be hard for me to believe, but we don't lie.

Marmar: No, I trust you two more than my eyes but it's hard to believe, you know?

Moon: This is a part of the photos we took.

Marmar: Wow, you really traveled to that decade. These photos and details are amazing.

Moon: So you finally believed.

Marmar: I believed that it was just a little strange and difficult for me because I have never had a close encounter with such a story.

Moon: We will travel together next time.

Marmar: We can do it now.

Moon: It's midnight now and is not enjoyable.

Sanaz: And don't forget that we bought tickets.

Marmar: Excitement effects.

Sanaz: No problem, I understand you very well.

Moon: Girls, my mom said it's time to sleep.

Sanaz: So good night. Tomorrow is a good day, we should be cheerful.

Moon: Good night. At this moment, Madusi called me.

Madusi: We didn't talk much in these days together.

Moon: Yes, and I miss talking to you.

Madusi: So, I have to do something. I change time and clock with my power. It's 11 o'clock at night.

Moon: Wow, you are very strong and smart.

Madusi: I want to talk to you about a few names today.

Moon: About names?

Madusi: Yes, about you and your mother real name is second Earth.

Moon: Maybe you don't believe it, but this is one of my most important questions.

Madusi: I believe you. Your real name is VAFA and you mother real name is NAZANIN and also you have elder siblings.

Moon: How interesting and lovely. But why didn't you tell me until now? Because you talked to me about many things.

Madusi: I told you before that I can't tell you everything in one time.

Moon: Oh, you're right. I forgot about it.

Madusi: You are getting more ready for the big change with each passing day.

Moon: I am ready for this big change.

Madusi: Yes, but you are not perfect yet and I will examine you mentally and spiritually.

Moon: While I was thinking about his words, I fell asleep.

Madusi: You are such an interesting person. I am talking to you and you are sleeping. But it's not a problem, tomorrow is an important day and we are going to have fun and we can talk later.

Sanaz: No, I do not think so.

Moon: What time is it?

Marmar: We thought you were dead.

Moon: You are very rude. I felt tired. And that's why I turned off my phone alarm.

Marmar: I was just joking. Maybe you forgotten the hockey.

Moon: No, I didn't forget, wait for me. As if Maryam was right, I felt like I died and I became alive. I will ask Madusi later, maybe he knows, but now we have more important things to do.

Sanaz: Don't be afraid; we have time. And we are not far from the stadium.

Moon: Shall we go?

Marmar: Excuse me, you are FLASH?

Moon: Yes, you are talking to Flash. We have to go before it's too late.

Sanaz: Because time passes quickly.

Moon: We talked together in the car and agreed that today is going to be a good day. And I cleared my mind of the superstition that when you are excited, everything is canceled and I don't think about it anymore.

Marmar: Finally, we arrived. Our beautiful stadium.

Sanaz: But Madison Square Garden is beautiful and here.

Moon: You two are like Tom and Jerry. Of course, I am also talking about bias.

Sanaz: Thank God that you accept. Give me the tickets.

Moon: I always accept. I always say that we should think about our behavior and see where we went wrong and try to change.

Sanaz: I feel that these are the effects of your friend.

Moon: You thought right.

Sanaz: I am really happy to see these changes.

Marmar: Girls, let's go inside.

Moon: We tend to keep talking till somebody stops us.

Sanaz: Another feature of ours.

Moon: We entered the stadium together while we were laughing.

Marmar: Home sweet home.

Moon: Credit to Lukita. After a few minutes, the match started and everyone was excited.

Marmar: We have to win. Otherwise I will be upset.

Moon: Don't worry and don't be afraid. We are very strong. At that moment, I saw Sanaz talk to someone. If I remember, after the match, I will ask her what happened.

Marmar: I was very stressed, but finally we won.

Moon: I wanna hug you. We won we are champion.

Sanaz: Champion?

Cris: Yeah, today is last match of the season.

Sanaz: Oh, I don't know.

Cris: You are not fan?

Sanaz: I am a New York Rangers fan.

Cris: What an interesting coincidence.

Sanaz: Wow, you are also fan, right?

Cris: Yes, I am here because of my sister.

Sanaz: Because of my friends.

Moon: Hey Sanaz, what are you doing?

Sanaz: I'm talking to this guy, his name is Cris and he is also Rangers' fan.

Moon: It's great. Nice to meet you.

Marmar: I liked his character.

Moon: Yes. Today, nothing can make me feel bad.

Sanaz: Wow and oh my God!

Marmar: What happened to you?

Moon: We were surprised by what had happened. What an interesting story!

Sanaz: It was as if we had known each other for years.

Moon: Pleasant talks.

Sanaz: He's fantastic.

Moon: After leaving the stadium, we went home together and said goodbye together on the same way.

Sanaz: I'll see you next week.

Moon: I was scared, I thought I forgot the key.

Madusi: But your mother has not gone anywhere.

Sanaz: But I know she is sleeping and I don't want to wake her up.

Madusi: How understanding!

Moon: Because I have a good teacher.

Madusi: You made me happy; I enjoy being with you and helping you.

CHAPTER ELEVEN

Moon: Although my friends can't see you, they understand your effects.

Madusi: So, they love me too.

Moon: Sometimes even more than me. After that, I went and slept because I felt tired.

Madusi: Well, now that the moon is asleep, I can go to the land and see if it's time for a big change or no.

•*Two weeks have passed since that night.*•

Mother: No, are you kidding?

Moon: It's true. Today also we wanna go to tunnel and travel in the time or I don't know.

Mother: Is it safe? Because I feel worried.

Moon: Mommy, look at these photos. We had traveled to the 80s with Sanaz and with Marmar to 50s.

Mother: You are very brave and courageous.

Moon: I was also stressed and afraid at first, but I believed in Madusi.

Mother: But really, I can't ignore Madusi's influence because I feel the changes myself and I am seeing you.

Moon: I'm glad you understand. It means a lot to me.

Mother: You are my lovely girl.

Moon: Mom, you can also call me Amaris.

Mother: What? Amaris?

Moon: Yes, if you want, I can explain for you.

Mother: I want but now I have too many works and also I heard the doors sound.

Moon: Finally, my friend came back.

Madusi: I saw happiness in her eyes.

Marmar: Amaris! How are you?

Moon: My favorite nickname. You don't know how much I missed you.

Marmar: Me too, darling. I brought you a gift from Netherlands.

Moon: Is it related to Van Gogh?

Marmar: I will never forget what Mrs. Smith said: You are very smart.

Moon: I love you my friend you are more than important to me.

Sanaz: You two don't want guests?

Marmar: You came on time and this is incredible.

Sanaz: I will definitely compensate for you in good time.

Moon: Tom and Jerry in the real world.

Marmar: I should not say that you are right, but I have to.

Moon: But now I'm eager to know more about Cris.

Marmar: I had completely forgotten about that story. She is right; explain.

Sanaz: We talk together about our personality, our interests and many things.

Moon: And you went to a coffee shop together twice.

Sanaz: Yes, and thank you for guiding me.

Marmar: We have a consultant here.

Moon: Girls, it's time to go.

Sanaz: Continued exploration in the 50s?

Moon: Yes, but I have a one idea. Let's travel together to 1962. And let's watch *Breakfast at Tiffany's* together.

Marmar: Oh, I'm so excited.

Sanaz: This is a great idea.

Moon: I asked Madusi and he did. Wow! Now we are in 1962.

Sanaz: How beautiful we have become!

Moon: No one will understand that we came from another era.

Marmar: We can also meet Elvis.

Moon: This is the most important point.

Sanaz: Girls, people are going where?

Moon: Now I'm thinking that it doesn't matter what movie we want to watch, the important thing is that we can experience cinema this year.

Marmar: I was waiting for you to say this.

Moon: The best decision we made was that we watched the movie together with other people.

Sanaz: This experience is even more unforgettable than the previous one.

Moon: Cars, people, cinema, theater, and everything in the most beautiful state.

Marmar: We have to consider the changes that have happened, but in I agree with you.

Moon: My next idea is we can go and bought get old cassettes

Sanaz: I admire your ideas. Look at that shop.

Moon: But we have to be careful with our behavior because they may doubt. I entered the store with my friends and asked the owner to allow us to take photos.

Mr. Johnson: Yes, you can take photos from my shop and also me.

Moon: After taking pictures of the items in the shop, we also took pictures with Mr. Johnson.

Marmar: He was very kind and loving and he was calmly explaining to us about his shop.

Moon: After that, we left Mr. Johanson's shop and started talking.

Sanaz: I liked his character. If we had time, we would listen to his words for hours.

Moon: We will come again, but now it's time to go back. We opened our eyes and realized that we were back at home.

Marmar: Again, an unforgettable and lasting experience.

Sanaz: Exactly, it was enjoyable full of good feelings. We would love to stay here, but we have a lot of work to do.

Marmar: Yes, Sanaz is right, my cousin's also came from Spain and I want to see them after many years, so good bye.

Moon: Good bye, I will definitely visit you. After my friends left, Madusi said that he wanted to tell me something.

Madusi: Now is the time to step into another period of evolution.

Moon: I have any idea about what you said.

Moon: I want you to open your eyes and give me your hand and don't be afraid at all.

Moon: I don't know what is going to happen, but I believe in you. As he said, I closed my eyes and felt some changes.

Madusi: Now you can open your eyes. Look in the mirror and see some changes.

Moon: I don't understand what happened. Where are we?

Madusi: You are now 25 years old and we are in California.

Moon: What? Is not unbelievable but I feel confused.

Madusi: But I feel confused.

Moon: My family? My friends.

Madusi: Don't worry, everything is the same as before.

Moon: I had a strange feeling, so I went out of my room and saw my father talking to my mother.

Dad: Good morning, Moon. Join us for breakfast. Our guests are arriving now.

Mother: I am glad that they also joined us.

Moon: Who are you talking about?

Dad: Your friends, Martin and Miller's family.

Moon: I want to go back to my room and start writing.

Mother: Everything is okay?

Moon: Yes, Mommy.

Dad: She behaved strangely.

Mother: Effects of changes.

Dad: Yes, you are right.

Moon: The feeling of not belonging to this space was driving me crazy.

Madusi: I feel like I have to make you calm down, so take this potion.

Moon: It's dangerous. I don't do it.

Madusi: It is not dangerous, listen to me.

Moon: I decided to listen to him. And suddenly I felt my feelings change. And I fell in love with the atmosphere where I was.

Madusi: The result of trusting me.

Moon: I always believed in your words and still do.

•*The first two weeks passed with a combination of strange and interesting feelings.*•

Lya: I knew I would be happy to meet you.

Moon: My feelings towards you are also mutual.

Sanaz: We are here.

Marmar: You met a new person, so please don't forget us.

Moon: I know your humor very well. BUT I love this squad. We are very similar to each other and this made communication easier.

Lya: A friendly and loving group but we hate each other.

Moon: Of course yes, our love language is annoy each other sometimes.

Sanaz: Maybe some people think that we should only love each other, but we don't think like that.

Lya: The most important point that should have been mentioned.

Moon: I agree with all of you But now I need my COFFEE.

Marmar: I know how you feel so hang on because I'll be right back.

Moon: I try to wait. I'm kidding. Let's talk about other things.

Lya: I miss Netherlands.

Moon: One of my favorite countries because of Van Gogh and Tulip especially.

Lya: Part of our identity. I will definitely go to my country on vacation.

Marmar: I have a great idea but I don't know.

Moon: Is it a strange idea?

Marmar: No, but our families are not going to agree.

Lya: I can guess. About RV and camper?

Sanaz: Girls, your coffees.

Marmar: Exactly yes.

Sanaz: Tell me what the topic of conversation is.

Lya: Travel together.

Sanaz: I love this idea but travel to where? With car?

Moon: With RV.

Sanaz: I love it more than anything.

Moon: we can talk about it later.

Lya: It's true. Let's enjoy the moment we have now.

Moon: After talking with my friends, we went to Lya's house I love your mother, she is very beautiful and lovely.

Lya: We love you too. Come with me. I wanna show you something.

Moon: You made me curious. Wait, what is this?

Lya: This is old gramophone. We are similar.

Moon: Wait Maybe you mean that you also know Abraham.

Lya: Yes, that's why I wasn't surprised when you talked about it.

Moon: By the way, I was very surprised at that time and I was thinking about it. How many years have you been talking to them?

Lya: Less than you, about six years.

Moon: We can talk a lot more about them.

Lya: I am glad that you are like me.

Moon: Finally, I said goodbye to Lya and I back to home and I saw my mother and she asked how was today? And I also said that it was a very good day and we had a lot of fun.

Mother: Everything is working out well and that's nice.

Moon: Mommy I ate dinner. And yes, I am happy too.

Mother: But I'm practicing a new dessert for Halloween.

Moon: What? Is Halloween near?

Mother: Look at the calendar.

Moon: Oh God. But I am not ready for it. What can I do now?

CHAPTER TWELVE

Mother: Try to be relaxed. We still have three days.

Moon: I quickly returned to my room and Madusi asked what happened.

Moon: I haven't done anything for Halloween yet.

Madusi: I fix everything in the best way.

Moon: Everything should be as beautiful as possible.

Madusi: I will not disappoint you.

Moon: My dear friend helped me and with his ideas. Everything changed in the most beautiful way possible and now it was time to sleep because I was very tired.

Madusi: As I said before, I have to go to the land ceremony.

Moon: We will talk together tomorrow.

Madusi: Getting to know them has been a divine favor and they are really different from the people I talked to before but now it is better to go to the land.

•*The days near Halloween, New York has a beautiful feeling. You see the people of the city getting ready for the celebration, people are working at home.*•

Moon: He was your brother?

Lya: Yes, and I wondered how you didn't recognize him.

Moon: It's getting more interesting by the minute.

Lya: Yes. Finally, we arrived and I think I found it.

Moon: Halloween costume's shop?

Lya: It's not just for Halloween. There are other costumes too.

Moon: I want to be Harley Quinn.

Lya: One of your great ideas and this also mind.

Moon: Favorite Cat Women.

Lya: We bought things. It is better to go to our house and see what is going on there.

Moon: No, I have a lot of work I'll come at night.

Lya: Your parents also want come to our house; my father invited them to be together tonight.

Moon: It was a nice surprise, so I went to their house with Lya and I met Theo for the first time.

Marmar: Look who's here, our beautiful friend.

Moon: Mirror, mirror.

Lya: What?

Moon: She said you are beautiful and I said I am a mirror and you see your own beauty in me.

Lya: You have a cool words and proverb in your language.

Moon: Oh thanks, Dutch also is wonderful. I want to decorate in my own style.

Sanaz: No, please no.

Moon: Trust me, I know what to do.

Sanaz: Just don't make it like that year.

Lya: Girls, what are you doing?

Moon: We are discussing and this story happened a few years ago when I wanted to make pumpkin but I messed up.

Theo: This time, yours will definitely be the best.

Moon: Thank you, I hope I don't mess it up.

Lya: He cares a lot about you.

Moon: Please don't say anything about it.

Marmar: Please explain it to us we are not strangers.

Moon: For now, let's focus on the celebration and decorations. Do you need help?

Lya: I have to go to the storeroom and get a white box.

Moon: I'm going to bring it.

Sanaz: Give it to me.

Moon: I went to a storage room and found that box just like Lya said and at that moment I heard Theo's voice. What are doing here?

Theo: I want to tell you something and this is very important to me.

Moon: Tonight, no because it's a very important night for me and I don't think about anything else except Halloween.

Theo: Okay, I respect your words but don't forget this, maybe we will meet each other in parallel worlds one day.

Moon: I went back to my friend without paying attention to what he said and we started doing things together and when we finished, we felt comfortable.

Lya: Good job, girls.

Marmar: We still have three hours.

Moon: I need some fresh air.

Lya: You can go to the greenhouse and feel calm.

Moon: I went to the greenhouse and started thinking.

Madusi: My friend, I feel that something is occupying your mind.

Moon: You guessed it right, I didn't behave properly, I shouldn't have ignored him. But these are not important Theo said something and my mind was confused.

Madusi: Meeting in the parallel world and the second Earth.

Moon: Do you know anything about him?

Madusi: Yes, but I can't tell you right now because the time has not come. And now I suggest you go back to your friends.

•At that moment, there was a commotion in the house.•

Lya: Tell me the truth, did you hurt her?

Theo: No, I just said I wanted to talk to you.

Lya: This is your biggest mistake because tonight is not good a time for that you wanted to say.

Theo: Your friend is back.

Sanaz: Try to stay calm and don't talk about it.

Moon: I tried to ignore him and think about preparing myself for tonight's party.

Lya: The house bell rang and the guests arrived.

Moon: Hello Mommy.

Mother: I love your custom Amaris.

Moon: Favorite maleficent.

Mother: I love our relationship.

Moon: We are close friends.

Theo: How happy her face was maybe there was a problem with me I don't anything right now.

Mother: Special thanks to your amazing family.

Lya: Auntie, you are so unique.

Mehrafarin: Happy Halloween to my bestie.

Marmar: They are so funny.

Lya: Everyone pay attention to me. We gathered tonight to celebrate Halloween once again but this time we are going to enjoy it together. So we light candles in the dark. Tonight, my mother is going to tell us one of the scary stories.

Moon: The story of the abandoned underground and the garden is one of my favorites in Halloween and while listening to it, I was both happy and scared.

Soraya: Now it's time to do another tradition.

Theo: The tradition of lighting the fire.

Moon: I also wanted to mention it.

Theo: What an interesting telepathy.

Nahid: Girls and boys, these are for you, a souvenir from tonight.

Theo: You are very tasteful.

Moon: My mother surprised us all and these gifts conveyed a very good feeling. After the party, we decided to watch a movie together in the yard with my friends.

Lya: Hocus Pocus is the best movie for now.

Moon: We all agree with you. After bringing it up, we went to the yard together and started watching the movie.

Sanaz: Suitable film meaning I love it. I love it.

Moon: Although it was one of my favorite movies, I felt strange in some scenes I felt scared but at the moment Theo told me that he is with me and not to be afraid. I still didn't know what to say, so I just smiled.

Madusi: I watched what was happening. It indicates the present and future tenses. It will happen in the coming days.

Madusi: I watched what was happening. It indicates the present and future tenses. It will happen in the coming days.

•*A week has passed since the party and Halloween and the relationship has become interesting.*•

Lya: Again us and again this coffee shop.

Moon: Here is my safe place I love it.

Lya: Oh, Theo and Simon are coming.

Sanaz: Hey bro what are you doing here.

Theo: Did we disturb you?

Lya: Yes, next question.

Moon: No, don't think like this. You know your sister more than me.

Theo: You are right. New book?

Moon: I decided to buy and read new books.

Theo: Your favorite character. Girls who love books are very attractive.

Lya: You forgot me again but don't get it wrong I'm joking with you.

Simon: The funniest person I have ever seen.

Moon: As always, we talked with my friend, shared memories and laughed and when I decided to go home Theo said he wanted to tell something.

Theo: Asterin, you know you are like a dream girl. And I know a dream girl should live in her dream world.

Moon: Who's that? I don't understand what you are saying.

Theo: Don't ask anything and listen. Getting to know you was very valuable for me and we will meet again.

Moon: I also said goodbye to him and was thinking about his words all the way.

Madusi: Hello, my friend, how was it today?

Moon: I don't know how to explain. I just feel confused.

Madusi: I know because I know everything about today and his words and he calls you Asterin. If you haven't forgotten, I was talking about it.

Moon: ASTERIN? Oh God! Maybe now is the time to change.

Madusi: Yes, you will understand. You got it right. Now you and your mother are ready, and don't worry, I mentally worked on her brain. And she's also ready like you.

Moon: I went to my mother and we closed our eyes and held each other's hands.

Madusi: We have now entered the tunnel together and you will be able to open your eyes and see everything in a few minutes.

Moon: I had a strange feeling as if I was going to be born again.

Mother: Hold my hand tight, I feel scared.

Moon: Don't be afraid and feel liberated.

Follow the pages to read parts of
second of this book series.

Way of Perfection and Life

Life flows in good and bad moments•

Madusi: Welcome HOME! They are waiting for you.

Nafise: How long I was waiting for you!

Vafa: Mommy Nafiseh, I am very happy to see you.

Nazanin: Family hug?

Nafise: Of course, yes, Alireza join us please.

Vafa: Mami Nafise showed me my room and said that she has been waiting for us for a long time.

Madusi: How do you feel now?

Vafa: To be honest with you, I don't know. But this change was not sudden. I was ready for it.

Madusi: I think it's time to go and meet your friends because they are back from a trip.

Vafa: Maybe my friends don't know me anymore.

Madusi: Don't worry and don't be afraid. They know you as if you were here with them for years.

Vafa: I informed Mami Nafiseh that I want to go and see my friends and she kindly accepted.

Nafise: But take care of yourself.

Vafa: Madusi is with me. I left the house and went to my friends as if everything was the same as before. They had not changed much.

Sanaz: This is my new friend Lya.

Lya: Hi, Vafa, my old friend.

Sanaz: I understand this is a secret between you.

Sanaz: Let's talk about our surroundings and pay attention to details.

Vafa: I think you forgot something.

Sanaz: Let me think. Oh yes, COFFEE!

Vafa: Love my life forever.

Sanaz: We are lucky because we are close to it.

Vafa: We also talk together.

Lya: We believed in seeing you again.

Vafa: We are the same people as before but in a different EARTH.

Lya: I know you feel alive now. You feel like you are reaching perfection.

Vafa: You talk like my friend. Madusi's words are like yours.

Lya: I know him very well and I'm glad he contacted you.

Vafa: I know you and it means a lot to me, like Madusi. You taught me many lessons and I want you to be with me.

Lya: I will always accompany you on the way to perfection and life.

Sanaz: I am back. Oh Vafa, I still can't believe that I saw you again.

Lya: Next week is first the day of college.

Vafa: I am ready for it more than anything.

Cris: Hello girls.

Vafa: How are you, Cris?

Cris: I'm fine and I just came back from a trip. I missed my sweetheart.

Sanaz: Of course, we were in contact with each other.

Cris: The real version is more valuable.

Sanaz: I accept your word because I feel the same way.

Cris: Are you ready for the first day of the new season in college?

Vafa: Ready? No more than ready.

Cris: So let's drink coffee together and wish to be happy.

Vafa: After that, I said goodbye to my friends and we returned home with Madusi. Every day that passes, you understand more about this environment and people are living here.

Vafa: Yes, I understand what you are saying. Wait, I have an important question.

Madusi: I know what you want to ask, so come with me.

Vafa: His power of understanding is very high. As soon as they entered the house, they ran to me and hugged me.

Omid: My little sister is back and this is absolute joy.

Bahar: She is our sister, not your sister.

Omid: I don't feel like arguing with you, so I won't say anything.

Vafa: In my opinion, enjoy this moment and don't argue.

Bahar: You are the most understanding person in our life.

Omid: Bahar give me my phone.

Bahar: Wait, boys' night?

Omid: With your Kamper.

Bahar: Mami Omid is very rude.

Nazanin: What's going on here?

Omid: I want to go out with my friends and I need that Kamper.

Nazanin: If you promise to be careful, I will let you.

Omid: I promise everyone that. Bahar, give me the key. Theo is waiting for me.

Vafa: That was the moment I felt confused I went back to my room and turned on the laptop And I decided to entertain myself, that was the best way I could think of.

Madusi: Are you sure this is the best way?

Vafa: I don't know anything right now. Please don't disturb me.

Madusi: Drink this tea to calm down.

Vafa: I'm not sure, but I'll drink it.

Madusi: Don't forget that trusting me will not disappoint you.

Vafa: I feel relaxed and liberated.

Bahar: Oh, you are here. I was looking for you.

Vafa: Has something happened?

Bahar: No, I just wanted to talk to you.

Vafa: I like it, but about what?

Bahar: About anything you can think of.

•*The boys' gathering was supposed to be a fun night.*•

Simon: Buy it from your sister.

Omid: Are you kidding me?

Simon: No, I am serious we can even travel with it.

Omid: I just realized what a smart person you are.

Cris: But I think Theo is not very well.

Theo: You are wrong, I am fine.

Cris: You are wrong, I am fine.

Omid: Theo! Give me that speaker.

Theo: Okay, don't forget my songs are unique.

Simon: Your music taste is my favorite.

• *A week is a good time to process and understand the surrounding environment.* •

Bahar: We do amazing things here and we are one of the best in the world. Oh, Papa Reza hello sorry I didn't know you were here.

Reza: How are you, my lovely girls?

Vafa: We are good. I came to see the company again. How big it is here!

Bahar: There are many things that I have to show you and tell you about.

Vafa: I am very excited for it all.

Bahar: Omid is calling; he must have returned home. Let's go have tea together and talk about many things.

Vafa: My whole being was filled with good feelings but little by little, I felt that the past is fading from my mind, as if I belonged here from the beginning.

Bahar: Are you okay? We arrived home.

Vafa: Oh, I was overthinking.

Bahar: You really look like me.

Omid: The best thing you did in your life it was trust to me.

Bahar: First Hello and second welcome back and third I was kidding. It is clear that I believe in you.

Vafa: Wednesday is the first day of university. But now I need to rest.

Omid: Sleeping is the thing in the world.

Vafa: I agreed with him and went to my room and I asked Madusi if my age has changed.

Madusi: Yes, this is also part of the changes that I talked to you about earlier.

Vafa: I feel good about tomorrow, but nothing is ready yet.

Madusi: This magic wand is yours. But be careful while using it.

Vafa: I can't believe that I was able to prepare things easily.

Madusi: We are going to do a lot of things together, but now it is better for you to rest.

Vafa: Yes, you are right. I felt that I was going to have a peaceful sleep after a long time, and it happened like this.

Lya: You look like a bear. I told you to wake up.

Vafa: Oh, good morning. What are you doing here.

Lya: I can't believe you forgot it what we said.

Vafa: No, I didn't forget, I was just a little tired.

Lya: You are really a bear, my dear.

Vafa: Wait for me. I will be back.

Lya: I got help from Madusi and we made her mind ready for this REUNION.

Vafa: I am ready and we can go out together. Are you talking to yourself?

Lya: Not always, only sometimes.

Vafa: Times Square is always crowded but we try to be calm.

Lya: I felt both good and bad at the same time and I was more interested in her reaction than anything else.

Vafa: Wow, I love this part of the world.

Lya: What do you think about coffee?

Vafa: My eternal love.

Lya: So wait for me to come back with coffee.

Vafa: I was paying attention to the details around me when I heard a voice.

Theo: I am glad to see you again.

Vafa: I can't believe it, oh my God! I told you that we are not saying goodbye.

Lya: I am back with coffee.

Vafa: So this was the plan.

Theo: to meet again in Times Square.

Vafa: I wanna hug you. You two are part my life and I feel very good now.

Lya: This makes us happy.

Vafa: We talked for long hours, laughed and even cried and these were part of the best moments. And finally, I returned home and told my sister about it.

Bahar: Yes, I knew about this story Madusi had spoken to me. But tomorrow is a very important day and it is better to think about it.

Vafa: Do you want to read the text of the speech?

Bahar: Yes, yes I like to read your writings.

Vafa: Bahar accepted what I wrote and said it was very good And I'm ready for tomorrow

Bahar: Vafa training is enough for now. Let's down go together.

Vafa: Did something happen?

Bahar: No everything is good. Mami said let's go to her.

Nafise: They are like us in every way.

Reza: I agree with you, Queen of our HOUSE.

Nafise: Politeness, personality, sobriety, beauty.

Vafa: Mami Nafise, we love you so much.

Nafise: Your feelings are mutual. Bahar, please bring that photo albums.

Bahar: Here you are!

Vafa: What old and beautiful photos!

Nafise: You know him?

Vafa: Elvis is one my favorite artist ever.

Reza: Your taste is extremely beautiful, my granddaughter.

Nafise: Another part of her personality.

Vafa: Mami Nafise showed me the rest of the old photos and they were full of beauty. After that, I practiced a few times to be ready for tomorrow.

Madusi: Do not tire yourself, we believe in you.

Vafa: I know but…

Madusi: I said enough; you need rest. You should be fresh tomorrow.

Vafa: Madusi was right, so I prepared all my things and slept.

Madusi: You should always listen to me. I'm joking.

Omid: What a heavy sleep! Sis, it's time to wake up.

Vafa: Who are you? Who am I?

Omid: Everything is okay?

Vafa: Oh sorry, bro.

Omid: No problem, go get ready. We have a lot of work to do today.

Vafa: Yes, you are right. I also have a speech.

Madusi: After everything was ready, they went to the university together.

•Fordham University… What a dreamy and beautiful place!•

Vafa: Oh, hi you also here.

Theo: Because of my sis and you. I'm sure you can do it in the best way.

Vafa: Thank you for coming.

Lya: Are you ready for it?

Vafa: Yes, I am ready to be my best.

Omid: The ceremony is starting.

Vafa: After Mr. Rodriguez's speech, it was my turn to go and speak. Mr. Rodriguez: Ms. Ebrahimi, we are all waiting for you.

Vafa: I felt good and started talking. I want to say that you should never give up on your goals and dreams. You may get tired, fail, and say that I will not continue. But think about what you want to achieve and who you want to be because the world needs all of us.

Bahar: I am proud of her more than anyone.

Vafa: After finishing the speech and talks, everyone cheered me.

Bahar: We always believe in you, dear.

Theo: Asterin, you are always perfect. You are part of destiny.

Lya: A name that means star and flower.

Vafa: I finally found the meaning of this word. You are also ANALOTE. It means the sun.

Vafa: I love and praise this fate with all my heart and for me, being is the most valuable.

SHAMAYEL ROIDEL

A young writer who linked the real world to fantasy and created a new dimension of fantasy and its combination with reality.